BEST MICROFICTION

2023

Series Editors
Meg Pokrass, Gary Fincke

Guest Editor
Deb Olin Unferth

BEST MICROFICTION 2023
 ISBN 978-1-949790-81-8
eISBN 978-1-949790-82-5

First Pelekinesis Printing 2023

For information:

Pelekinesis
112 Harvard Ave #65
Claremont, CA 91711 USA

ISSN 2641-9750

www.pelekinesis.com

*Best
Microfiction
2023*

Best Microfiction Anthology Series

Series Editors
Meg Pokrass, Gary Fincke

Guest Editor
Deb Olin Unferth

Copy Editor
Michelle Christophorou

Production Editor
Cooper Renner

Layout and Design
Mark Givens

Cover illustration
Terry M. Givens

TABLE OF CONTENTS

BEST MICROFICTION

ESSAYS & INSIGHTS

FOREWORD

MEG POKRASS AND GARY FINCKE,
SERIES CO-EDITORS

Here we are, in 2023, and robots seem to not only have taken over the world, they've threatened to abolish our uniqueness as literary writers. This year, for the first time ever, we're seeing an onslaught of literary magazines now accepting submissions from A.I. bots. Even a year ago, this kind of scenario would have been unthinkable.

It is our opinion that now is the best time in the world for writers to push back and continue to develop their human craft. To do so in spite of the fact that the world seems to have fallen happily, willingly, into the arms of robot replacements. A.I. may trick us with its ever-sophisticated mimicry, but it won't ever allow us a sense of fulfilment as artists.

Here at *Best Microfiction*, our small staff continues to be an A.I. free team . . . Our writers and editors have human eyes, all-too human bodies, and warm, creative hearts. And though, as an editorial team, we may not always be able to tell what is A.I.-generated writing from what is genuine human writing, we encourage our writers to trust both their own brains and their hearts.

Let this collection of offbeat, quirky, one-of-a-kind gems, so carefully selected from thousands of stories published in 2022, stand as proof that the creative spirit in us flawed, human writers can survive the coming onslaught of artificial literature.

INTRODUCTION

DEB OLIN UNFERTH, GUEST EDITOR

What is the smallest space that a story could fit?
The fewest number of words? Consider this one by
Gertrude Stein.

LONGER
She stayed away longer.

Is this a story? I've always loved how the title and
last word create ironic bookends, how this tiny
five-word piece gives off a spark of yearning, impa-
tience, suspense. Why did she stay away? Who is
waiting for her to return? The microshort is about
gesture, hint, word choice, imagination. I thought
about that, as I read through the hundreds of terrific
submissions in order to select the stories for this
collection. I found in the smallest spaces true beauty
and everything that moves me in microfiction:
formal invention, a spirit of revolution, playfulness,
passion, strangeness, ambiguity, mystery. I found
stories that slip into philosophical reflection with a
turn of phrase, stories that experiment with sound
and repetition and syntax. I encountered immense

emotional complexity and explorations of where humanity might be headed, the visions ranging from dour to soaring.

Microfiction strikes me as the closest prose may come to an authentic copy of an artist's inner rhythm and chatter. This collection reads to me like dozens of individual heartbeats, all different, all making their own urgent sound.

BEST MICROFICTION

ATTABOY LOUIS

SHASTRI AKELLA

Louis liked the name: Prospect Cemetery. As if its prescient eighteenth-century builders had known that one day college boys would come there to look for one-night boyfriends.

Louis himself found no prospects in Prospect Cemetery. He tried but they didn't find him pretty. He sat on the branch of an apple tree and relished the collective ruckus of their pleasure. They didn't mind; he cleaned up after they left.

One day, he lingered on the trash of the boy he loved but couldn't have. Gus Pitman, senior, kinesiology. He wanted to pocket Pitman's condom, he longed to eat the leftovers of the pizza that Pitman had bitten into with his perfect teeth.

Pitman *actually* talked to Louis one night: he zipped his trousers up, clapped Louis on the back and asked, "How's it going?"

Louis replied that he hated winter nights.

"I guess I'll see you around," Pitman said as he stood there shirtless and smoothed his ginger 'stache down with his thumb.

Back in his dorm, Louis locked himself in the bathroom and cried. His tears, hot with delight, made him crave apples.

On winter nights when Prospect Cemetery was full of snow and empty of boys, Louis stayed in his bed and pictured framed photographs on his room's bare walls. In those photos he was married and had a husky by his side. Pitman's favorite breed.

Louis always threw the trash away: he never brought the condom home, he never ate the crust. Louis may have seemed ugly to the cemetery lover boys, but he believed in consent.

Shastri Akella's debut novel, *The Sea Elephants*, is forthcoming from Flatiron Books. His fiction has appeared in *Guernica*, *Fairy Tale Review*, *The Master's Review*, and elsewhere.

EL DELIVERYBOY

CHRISTINE ARROYO

Asphalt and steel, trash piled Empire State Building high, taxi cabs out to kill you, pedestrians that taunt you crossing the street against the light, gunmen on motorcycles trying to steal your electric bike—your lifeline, your everything, you saved for that bike one two-dollar tip at a time, you've tricked it out—LED color-changing strip lights on the rear rack, Honduras flag flying blue and white, stars swishing in the frigid wind, racing from Washington Heights to Industry City—someone wanted a Filipino pastry for eight dollars, you stand there in the rain, waiting for them to answer the buzzing intercom, you discover there's no elevator and hike up four flights of stairs, dripping wet, hand over the pastry bag, guy calls you a hero but won't look you in the eye, no tip, you race back down to your bike praying it's still there—it is, thank god—insulated backpack with more deliveries clanging against your back—it's 11 pm, four more hours to go—all these people who never have to leave their apartments, swaddled in blankets, Netflix and food handed to them in bags, the furthest they ever have to walk is to their front door—you've given yourself the goal of making ten thousand deliveries this year, maybe then you'll be like the guy up in apartment 504—on your couch pushing buttons on your phone, food appearing out of nowhere, more like sending money home for your wife and daughter, maybe one day they'll be able to join you, but for now you race on your bike—wind, sleet, rain slapping against your face, arms aching, back cramping, Honduras flag flying, they call you El Deliveryboy en la Gran Manzana delivering an ice cream cone in the middle of Hurricane Ida—furious wind knocking your bike from side to side, handlebars nearly ripped from your hands, you don't worry about your life, your safety, or construction beams flying across and decapitating you—you worry about the ice cream cone in the insulated pack, is it melting, are the sprinkles still there, has it fallen off its cone?

Christine Arroyo's work has been published in *X-R-A-Y Literary Magazine*, *Flash Fiction Magazine*, *Dark Recesses Press*, *Beyond Words*, and *Variety Pack*, to name a few. She has just completed her first novel about siblings navigating an increasingly warming world.

HOME

MATT BARRETT

Our mother drives us to the home where she was raised. It has fallen, mostly: the roof is torn so its beams are all the vultures see as they glide in figure eights, which my sister says means infinity. The porch sinks into a patch where tomatoes grew, but what remains is a pile of children's toys and bikes with rusted fenders and plywood ripped from the walls with nails bent like the backs of old men. It looks as if a storm blew through, but there was no storm. No tornado or hurricane—no, nothing like that. When our mother left this place, to live with a man she no longer knows, her parents begged her to stay. But she went, to live in canyons and rivers, in rolling fields the farmers threshed at dawn. She buried her hands in soil, covered her face in dirt, and howled at tractor trailers illuminating the sky. She says, "There is no story here," when we ask her what she remembers. Above us, the vultures glide. My sister repeats, "Infinity," and a teapot sings from inside. Our mother scales the porch, enters the kitchen. The stove is on, and her mother is standing there in her bathrobe. We have never met her. "Claudette?" she asks. Sun shines through the open beams. It lightens our mother's hair, her skin. She sits at the only table, among the pile of rubble. There are no walls dividing rooms, no floors but stacks of wood, no home except for what she remembers. Her father opens the back door, kisses our mother's head. Grease stains line his arms, his shirt. He sits with her at the table and reads the paper. The house smells of butter and syrup, even from out here. Our mother's mother joins them, smiles at us through the wall. They reach for their forks, their napkins, and eat.

THE BEACH

MATT BARRETT

He remembers they took their father's truck, so they had room for all their things. He remembers a curve on the highway, in either New York or Connecticut, and a high concrete wall hiding the sun and trees. He remembers getting there—sitting in the backseat, the belt across his chest. He remembers no one saying much. His father parking the truck and shutting his eyes, leaning the driver's seat so far back Joanne had to sit in the middle. He remembers his father snoring, and his mother whispering, "It's been a long day," as if they hadn't lived through it, too. He remembers stepping out of the truck and walking through the parking lot. And seeing the beach at the end of a ramp and footprints in the sand and children screaming at each other to play. He remembers sitting down beside Joanne. Not on the beach but at the edge of the parking lot. He remembers watching the ocean from there. In his mind, it is just a collage of yellow and blue and white. He remembers Joanne shouting, "Whale!" and his heart beating faster than he knew it could, before she added, "You must have missed him, he must have swam away." He remembers looking for more of them—whales, dolphins, seals. Anything. He remembers how the smells were different, how the air was different, how it seemed like the world either started or ended here, how everything met at this one small place, the land converging with the sea.

He doesn't remember the panic in his mother's voice, when she shook him awake to pack, or the sound of men shouting a moment before. He doesn't remember a woman at the Sunoco mouth, "My God," when his father stepped out to pump gas or when he decided his father was someone to fear. He doesn't remember his mother shushing Joanne to calm down or his father scrubbing blood and bone from the cracks in his hands at a rest stop in New Jersey. When he thinks about that day too hard, it feels more like a dream, a blur of colors and nothing more. But he still remembers they made it. He still feels it: the air and mist and his heart beating as he followed Joanne's finger to a part of the world where even giants could disappear.

Matt Barrett is a writer from Pennsylvania. He teaches creative writing at Gettysburg College and holds an MFA in Fiction from UNC-Greensboro. His work has appeared or is forthcoming in *The Sun Magazine*, *The Threepenny Review*, *The Baltimore Review*, *SmokeLong Quarterly*, *Wigleaf*, and elsewhere.

FROM YOYO

JANELLE BASSETT

I learned the word fuck from a girl named Yoyo. She
told me fucking was when you lift your shirt up all
the way and I believed her because she talked a lot
more than I did and because she had a brother and
I didn't. We were four or five, out on the daycare
playground, pretending that our horses were eating
the sand from the sandbox. It made them strong to
eat the sand but it also made them sneezy. They had
those big honking horse nostrils, after all. Sand traps.
We played that their saddles kept being knocked
off by the force of the sneezes, so we'd bend over to
pick up the far flung saddles and put them back on
our horses' backs and then pat their firm, invisible
rumps. We had run around and bent over so many
times that we were hot and red, so Yoyo was like,
"I'm sweaty. Let's go over in the shade and fuck."

She went under the tree and lifted her shirt all
the way up. She couldn't see me with her shirt like
that so she yelled, "Are you doing it too?" I didn't
want to do it too because my cousin told me that
my belly looked like it had a dead baby in it and I

17

wanted to keep that shape a secret, but she was the only person who played with me consistently and didn't seem to mind that I hardly ever spoke—that I mostly nodded and smiled and made that rabbit-teeth face—so I didn't want to leave her to fuck alone under the daycare tree. I joined her, and we really did cool down like that. Shade for the face, air for the belly.

Yoyo said that the horses smelled the salt on our bellies and were licking our skin, so we laughed and squirmed and told them to stop because we were their owners, respectable and responsible. But really we loved the attention. Or Yoyo loved it and I did my best to imagine what loving it would be like.

Janelle Bassett's writing appears or is forthcoming in *The Rumpus*, *New Delta Review*, *SmokeLong Quarterly*, *The Offing*, *Washington Square Review*, *Wigleaf* and *River Styx*. She lives in St. Louis and is a Fiction Editor at *Split Lip Magazine*.

VISITACION VALLEY, 1962

PATRICIA Q. BIDAR

It won't be long before Maisie brings out that one framed photo. The one of her in her Valentine's dress, white with a wide red sash. She holds a velvet purse that she'd borrowed from her cousin. She'd spent half an hour ratting up her hair. Made up her face before her bath. The bouffant nearly touched the mounted deer that decorated their kitchen wall.

The mounted deer head was looking down. Dell's first kill, from his teenage days. Maisie's face was round and flushed. She'd just finished her martini, and she held a briny pimiento-stuffed olive in one cheek.

Sweet Dell taking Maisie's picture, his mouth open in concentration. Afterward, Maisie playing her concertina for him. Lost in their world of dress-up, cocktail food, and television westerns. Their favorite, set in New Mexico, was about a New Mexico rancher and his boy.

For dessert, Maisie would wiggle the Jell-O from its mold, treating herself to miniature marshmallows from the bag. She'd let them dissolve in her mouth.

Such free, glide-y times. The things she learned from him. To massage his feet until he fell asleep. To perform acrobatics in their bed which she laughed to think about during the day while he was at work. To shoot a .270 Weatherby Magnum.

She and her Dell, natural as forest animals. Jellyfish bobbing in turbulence-free currents. Easy as umbrellas floating down from the sky. Maisie'd let her friend-ships slide away. And then Dell himself, so much older, had slid away. She lives in a furnished mobile home now. Half Moon Bay. A magical-sounding place. She took little from their home. Just the photo, Dell's watch, the gun.

Patricia Q. Bidar is a third-generation Californian from the Port of Los Angeles area. An alum of the U.C. Davis Graduate Writing Program, she also holds a degree in Filmmaking. Patricia's stories are included in numerous journals and anthologies including *Flash Fiction America* (W.W. Norton, 2023). Visit her at https://patriciaqbidar.com.

HOLY WAR

BRETT BIEBEL

A kid from our town fell off the water tower and walked away. 150 feet and no hospital, no fractures, not a fucking scratch, and media were everywhere. Must've been a slow news week. Trucks from Fox and ABC News, and they're interviewing all these Big Ten physicists who keep talking about subatomic particles and many worlds and statistical improbabilities, and some of these real fundamentalist-type churches set up tents on site, and you could sometimes hear them singing. Praise and worship shit. Steven Curtis Chapman or whatever. A few of them put up this massive cross on the exact spot, and this was after the whole thing died down. Everyone left, and the kid went back to drinking and driving down to Iowa to bet on hockey and baseball, and sometimes me and Maggie will head out there at night. To the cross. It's strung up with Christmas lights the whole year round. Was a big fight at some city council meeting a while back about power supply and public expense, but then this private donor came through, and it's like Jesus turning water into wine how these farm town Christians can always get their hands on some serious scratch, and we like to drink wine out there now that I mention it. The nice bottles. Ten, twelve bucks and just dry enough, and we talk about miracles. Money. The whole thing's purple and giant and gold, and I ask Maggie what she believes in.

"Kids," she says. "Crops. Anything that grows, and what about you," and I never have an answer. Too complicated. The way miracles are nothing but tiny numbers, and I'd get my ass back up there if I was him. Stare straight down. Measure an arc. Linger on choosing and death and significance, and what are the odds, I'd think. The chances I could somehow pull it off again.

Brett Biebel's short fiction has appeared in dozens of literary journals, including *SmokeLong Quarterly*, *Wigleaf*, and *The Masters Review*. He is also the author of *48 Blitz* (Split/Lip Press, 2020) and two forthcoming flash fiction collections. His readers' guide to Thomas Pynchon's *Mason & Dixon* will be released by University of Georgia Press in 2024.

TATTOOS

JAMY BOND

We didn't tell anyone. Not our parents, not our friends, and Jethro cared only about the cash in our pockets, not that we were fourteen.

We lived in a Florida port town where heat was like a second skin, a bear suit you had to wear. In August, the humidity could mess with your head, make you think you were drowning.

Our moms drank Tab and did Jazzercise and worried that we might be gay. They didn't want our lives to be difficult. They had no idea that on weekend nights we slipped from our bedroom windows and walked to the Club Detroit on 2nd Street where we drank rum and Cokes and danced to Psychedelic Furs songs. Sometimes, we French-kissed the sailors on shore leave. Most of them had wives; they just wanted our tongues for a few minutes. It never got scary or real.

And then one night your dad cornered me in the backyard while you were inside playing Frogger. We used to laugh at him, how he'd come home from a ten-mile run and crack open a beer, sweat streaming down his face. He was like a cartoon character. A Dad who did dumb Dad things.

Suddenly your mom had a boyfriend named David and you were moving to the other coast and it felt like our lives were ending, our hearts exploding, the adult world closing in.

We picked two Siamese cats and Jethro fired up his ink gun. It sounded like a chainsaw. I wanted orange eyes; you wanted green. It would be our little secret, forever hidden beneath the rim of our pants.

I went first.

Does it hurt? you asked.

It feels like a bee sting, I said, wincing. *Sun blisters.*

And I remembered your dad watching us from the kitchen window while we sunbathed on green jelly chairs, our bikini tops untied to avoid tan lines, baby oil to soak up the rays.

Jamy Bond's stories and essays have appeared in a variety of print and online publications, and been nominated for Best of the Net, Best Microfiction, Best American Essays, Best American Short Stories and the Pushcart Prize. She is a Co-Editor-in-Chief at *SugarSugarSalt Magazine.*

A PIECE OF YOU

DIAMOND BRAXTON

I've successfully made my first pot of gumbo following the recipe you left me. I chew on andouille sausage and see you cutting links into perfect slices. Your brown hands are steady and never shake. When you disappear, I break apart a crab leg and suck down the savory Cajun broth. You reappear, and this time you are showing me how to eat a crab leg for the first time. I pick it up and feel the brittle boned shell and gag. You smack my hand playfully and take it from me. "Like this," you say patiently as you break it in half as if it were a lead pencil.

Next, I take a bite of shrimp, and we're at the grocery store. Three types of shrimp stare back at us. I pinch my nose because it smells like deep sea. I look at you, waiting to see which one you'll pick. Then you turn to me. "Which one you want?" I squint at the options and reply, "Whichever will allow me to have more." You laugh at that. "That's my ladybug."

I slurp down the broth and watch as memories flood my vision. You are sixty-two and breaking apart pecans from the tree in the front yard, you are seventy and are frustrated with your new wheelchair, you are ninety and crying when I tell you I'm getting married.

When the bowl is finished, a fullness takes over. There's still so much gumbo left. I set some aside for myself and pack the rest into separate Tupperware. Then I call the family and tell them I'm bringing over a piece of you.

Diamond Braxton is a queer, mixed-race Black-Chicana writer and editor pursuing an MFA at Texas State. Her work appears in *The Forge Literary Magazine*, *Stanchion*, *Hellebore Press*, and others. She's the Editor-in-Chief for *Defunkt Magazine* and a Copy Editor for the *Porter House Review*.

WARMER WATER

MATHIEU CAILLER

It's our first day together since the divorce, my daughter and me, and I'm picking her up for a visit. A new kind of dad now. I don't wake up with her in the other room. I don't make her eggs with toast buttered on both sides. Now, I make plans before I see her. I am, in a sense, something of a playdate. Only there for a few hours on the weekends.

I'm taking Abigail whale watching. She has wanted to go for a long time, and I have pushed it aside until today, a cold day in Los Angeles, with the sun out, but the wind equally present.

She is dressed in her new Converse sneakers I sent her by mail, but she does not mention them, and I do not point them out.

We head off on the ship named Serenity, and she eats some sour cherry gummies, a couple at a time, transferred quickly from her hoodie's hand-warming pouch to her mouth. Most times, I would tell her no, but I pretend I do not see things now.

The ship stirs and pushes farther into the Pacific. From here, on the bow, we stand, staring back at it all. The world, becoming blurry with distance.

The P.A. system crackles, and the guide tells us to be on the lookout to the north, that the gray whales will be streaming from Alaska to Mexico, in search of warmer water. And that whales have a sort of auto-pilot system that allows them to shut off portions of their brain while still swimming forward. I think that sounds perfect.

Abigail tugs on my shirt sleeve. She points to the horizon and tells me she sees one. Others nearby pick on her cues and do their best to locate the mammal, but all I see is a riptide, eddying in a beautiful spot of sun, reflecting and refracting light, and I stare at that instead. Isn't it something? she says. And I have to agree.

Mathieu Cailler is the author of six books. His most recent is the novel, *Heaven and Other Zip Codes*, winner of the LA Book Festival Prize.

CAT BARBECUE

TIM CRAIG

In years to come, this is how Dayna and Greg will refer to it and when they do, their friends will give them strange looks and say things like "you barbecued a cat?" and "the hell did it taste like?" which will make the two of them roll their eyes. But right now, they are still young and they are here, drinking beer, and their host's cat is weaving in and out of their legs in that seductive, electric way cats do. The hot fat from the grill has yet to drip off the grill onto the cat's back, causing it to dart in terror through the fence out into the road where the laundry truck—driven by a guy called Ricky who is on his phone, but who probably wouldn't have been able to stop in time anyway—has yet to appear. Greg has his strong arm around Dayna, his right thumb teasing the underneath of her breast through the material, the breast that, years from now, will be the source of the trouble not even his strong arm will be able to fix, and he'll wonder if he shouldn't have felt something all those years earlier—maybe even at the Cat Barbecue—because these things, he has read somewhere online, start long before you know. But Dayna will get irritated and say if *I* didn't know back then, how the fuck were *you* supposed to know? Though that's all for the future, and right now it is just a barbecue, not yet even the Cat Barbecue, and the cat is weaving in and out of their legs in that seductive, electric way, and the moon is high and everyone is young.

Tim Craig lives in London. A winner of the Bridport Prize for Flash Fiction, his short-short stories have appeared twice previously in the *Best Microfiction* anthology. His debut collection, *Now You See Him*, was published in 2022 by Ad Hoc Fiction.

KNOCKING

TOMMY DEAN

on doors in the middle of the night had become essential. We weren't sleeping, anyway. Blood spiked with sugar from shotgunning cans of Mountain Dew, *Beavis and Butt-Head* was too stupid even to laugh at. Truth or Dare meant nothing when we already told each other everything, so the dare at every Saturday sleepover was the knocking.

After midnight, we cut the music, dropped the lights, and lay head to head, shoulders covered by neon-colored nightgowns, while our legs sweated beneath the twin fabrics of our leggings and the shimmery padding of our sleeping bags. We practiced calming our breathing, hearts hammering, waiting for Gwen's or Justina's mom to do the final check before they drifted down the hall to their own beds. The dads plodded down the hall, never stopping at the bedroom door, never saying goodnight.

A year ago, Kelsey's dad sat on the corner of her bed at one in the morning and sang us love songs, his voice weepy, his busted knuckles creaking as he gripped the comforter. We didn't go out that night. We kicked and elbowed each other, keeping everyone awake, not knowing what would happen if we all fell asleep. Eventually his voice hitched, and he whispered, *Goodnight now, goodnight.* Kelsey apologized, said he just missed her mom, said it wasn't fair that he was so sad, and could they just go to sleep? Everyone nodded and faked sleep, until dawn, each of us calling our own mothers, asking to come home.

Kelsey was no longer invited. We didn't have time for sadness, for unpredictable fathers, for Saturday nights spent sleeping. We had to knock and shriek and run and hide behind mailboxes and China grasses that had grown willowy at the edge of winter-split driveways first paved in the 60s. Only here were we brave enough to face these men, our fathers and neighbors, their legs naked but dusted with hair, stomachs rounded from stress and beer, hair sprouted in different directions, their arms lifted in fists, striking out at invisible phantoms. Bewildered and angry, from a distance, they had never looked so safe.

THE ROMANTIC MANEUVERS OF A TILTING PLANET

TOMMY DEAN

Before the car was repossessed, before the house was sold at auction, before our father lost his job, and before our mother started living in the hotel 6 that she cleaned twelve hours a day, six days a week, before the youngest of us was born, before the emergency room visits, before the diagnosed panic attacks, before 9/11, before smoke and jet fuel became molten heat, before the war, yes that war, with its victimized civilians, and their voices curdled by the accumulating smoke and dust, before the second of us was born, our parents met at an art museum, both of them drawn to the light and loneliness of that Hopper painting. Their hands meeting like leaves falling onto the same patch of ground, their ends curling toward each other. Strangers kissing like newlyweds, a photo that hangs in our parents' bedroom, gathering dust, knocked askew by our play fighting. The times that always lead to bloody noses and bruised eyebrows. The only time we can get our father to sit with us, his hands wrapped around an ice pack, his other arm around our shoulders, the smell of melted metal and grease, a smokiness we inhale and hold in our chests, promising him that our mother will return. That before is just a dot on the timeline of their love.

Tommy Dean is the author of two flash fiction chapbooks *Special Like the People on TV* (Redbird Chapbooks, 2014) and *Covenants* (ELJ Editions, 2021), and a full flash collection, *Hollows* (Alternating Current Press 2022). He lives in Indiana where he currently is the Editor at *Fractured Lit* and *Uncharted Magazine*.

DAD PADDLES IN

TEDDY ENGS

When Dad paddles in I'm like thank God, no more sitting alone on this stupid beach, no more squinting against the violent sea-glare, no more trying to will him from his endless catch-a-wave-then-paddle-back-out cycle, counting down from ten, counting up from one, pleading let this be the last one let this be the last one each time a wave suggests itself on the horizon, but now, as Dad bellyrides the white-water, dismounts in the shallows, marches against the yanking tide, I imagine the car ride home, the questions about why I quit so early, why I look like I'm about to cry, I imagine the smack of his first beer, the stink of his eighth, and wonder if there is a way to freeze the moment when he has crested his final wave, sits contemplating whether to go for one more or call it for the day, then actually calls it for the day, I wonder if there is a way to freeze that exact moment and make it my Dad, my whole Dad, a Dad who's constantly paddling towards, but never reaching me.

Teddy Engs is a writer and musician living in Portland, Oregon. His work has appeared in *Swamp Pink*, *Split Lip Magazine*, and *Chestnut Review*.

THAT VASECTOMY TALK

SEAN ENNIS

Grace and I were having that vasectomy talk, when one of the dogs walked in, and of course, with him, there had been no conversation. I get the sense that I'm supposed to be elegiac. Surgery is dangerous, but I take it as natural that as I get older, I will start to lose abilities, even now, and already. I have already been a father.

I saw Gabe in his bloody beginnings.

"Nothing will change," Grace said. She was wearing a T-shirt, no bra. I'd like to believe her. Plus, I'm all for change if that's part of the deal. Sometimes, it shocks me that I even still live in this town. I used to like adventure, my history suggests. I've seen both oceans. And the Gulf.

"It doesn't hurt," Grace said. That sounded nice.

"There will still be pleasure," Grace said, but how could she know, is my body so obvious?

I just searched for "urologists near me" and scheduled a consultation. Probably, I wouldn't have to take my pants off. My Patreon subscribers would love this content. The doctor studied at Penn.

The fireworks were decent at the Watermelon Carnival that night, but there was a heavy police presence. The crowd brought their guns to the seed-spitting contest. We met a stressed out emotional support dog in the crowd, and we saw friends. My conversation skills were coming back, but I didn't bring it up. Everyone had new jobs to talk about on the patio, and dead loves.

I'd recently been accused of wife-worship. No, I did not say swapping. What would I want with your wife? People are not like—do you remember?—baseball cards. But what Grace says, more than likely, goes.

Still, I can't get over the feeling something is in need of puncturing, or of being pinched off, or of closing down.

Sean Ennis is the author of *Cunning, Baffling, Powerful* (Thirty West) and *Chase Us: Stories* (Little A). He lives in Mississippi and more of his work can be found at seanennis.net.

EVERYTHING DEPENDS ON THE POTATO

EPIPHANY FERRELL

Lou thinks it looks like a baby. I don't. If we can do something with this potato, if we can win a world record with this giant, then that'll be something. Lou will be happy.

At 17 pounds, it's not even a baby. It's a small child.

I choose a dress for the dog. I started putting dresses on Peanut a few months ago. To make Lou happy. This one is pink, with a poodle embroidered on the skirt. A poodle skirt for a Chihuahua. That's okay, isn't it? I'll see if Lou notices.

"That's my baby girl," he says to the dog. "That's my princess. Tell Mommy you need a pancake."

I never mastered pancakes. Mine are flat and heavy and the syrup sits on top of them. I do my best.

"Tell Daddy if he goes to the store, we need milk," I tell Peanut, turning a fresh pancake from the electric skillet.

This is how we talk now, through the dog.

Lou goes to the back bedroom, fetches the 17-pound

potato, puts it in the highchair he nabbed when the neighbor put it out for trash. He cuts up pancake, puts it on the tray in front of the potato.

I can't tell him about the letter, the one from the world record people. Our potato is not a potato. They don't say what it is, but potato it is not. DNA stuff. I don't know what that means. Or how they got DNA. I'm afraid to ask Lou.

"Ask Daddy if he wants to come to the park," I say to Peanut.

Peanut barks.

"Tell Mommy we'll get our shoes," Lou says.

He'll push the potato in the kiddie swing, and he'll smile.

JACK AND JILL'S FINAL ADVENTURE

EPIPHANY FERRELL

They hadn't told anyone about Jack's cancer. Not officially. Jill had known. Of course. She was there when he got the call, there to see him set his phone down on the table, missing it, the phone clattering to the kitchen floor.

"They called? On the phone. They could have had you come into the office, talked to you face to face," she'd said, angry about protocol. Jack understood that Jill felt helpless, that her protective instinct had to go somewhere.

Of course, there was chemo. Jill had dark circles under her eyes, and Jack protested, ordering her to take better care of herself.

"We're twins."

"Don't shave your head to match, too," Jack tugged on her ponytail for the sake of tradition.

Prostate cancer moves fast. The first round of chemo failed. Jack didn't want a second round. There wasn't much point.

They spent their last Christmas together in Vermont, at their grandparents' old farm, turned now into an Airbnb by the new owners. There was snow on the ground when they arrived and four inches overnight. "Snow day," they exclaimed, watching a snowmobile go by on the road.

They remembered the way to the hill as if it hadn't been fifteen years since they'd been there. There was the sledding slope. And there, just yards to one side, was the slope with the deadly drop-off.

They had their vintage Flexible Flyers, purchased from eBay. In great shape, too. They'd sand-papered the rust off the runners the night before. They'd bucketed water to the hill early in the morning, making ice. "Fast," they said to each other.

They poised the sleds at the top of the hill, Jack on one slope, Jill on the other. The thin layer of ice gleamed rosy in the late afternoon sun. Jack's eyes were luminous in his chemo-ravaged face. Jill's eyes were filled with all the things they would never do together.

"Race you!" Jack cried, leaped onto his sled, and away he went! Fast as lightning. He looked over his shoulder once to see if he was winning.

Jill watched him go, airborne, flying. She positioned her sled, barely able to see the sled tracks on the drop-off slope. And she went tumbling after.

Epiphany Ferrell lives on the edge of the Shawnee National Forest in Southern Illinois. Her stories appear in more than sixty journals and anthologies, and she received the Prime Number Magazine Flash Fiction Prize in 2020. Visit at epiphanyferrell.com or on social media.

VIA COMBUSTA

SARA FETHEROLF

This is the season girls go missing, sleeping in beds not their own.

One bolts awake, speaking a dead language. One is drinking bad wine from the bottle in a floodwater parking lot. She raises her collar like wolf hackles against the cold.

The band paid one to lie in a beautiful coffin all Halloween night as they played their show, red-nailed hands crossed neat over the heart. She is bleeding on schedule, & she is silent. Her black lace dress won't show a stain.

One is the moon, who travels the sorcery road this time of year. One is a heart, & one is a red nail. One is the key to her mother's old house. She will bleed when she's set in a lock without permission. She is on schedule, silent.

One is taking a shortcut between towns when the radio cuts out—then in the after-hiss, her own voice wobbles through, asking a question she can't pick up. The freaked flare of a fox splits the road—she swerves too fast & catches a skid—the high school's lit sign whips by (*TIME MANAGEMENT CLASSES*).

This is the way—snow bends into star—the road unfolds, opens, becomes, suddenly, full of girls. Their eyes, multiplicitous in the dark windshield, are flames/ keys/ hers, suspended mid-swerve.

Then just as quick, the wheel is back in her control; the road beneath her; animal safe on the other side. The static cuts in, spangled & talismanic: her own heart, thrumming.

The voice is gone. She waits to hear it again.

Sara Fetherolf is the author of *Via Combusta*, winner of the 2021 New American Press Poetry Prize. They have an MFA degree from Hunter College, and are a PhD candidate in Literature and Creative Writing at USC. They live in Long Beach.

A SOLID CONTRIBUTION

KATHY FISH

We have failed at Lincoln/Douglas debate. We have failed at Speech. We have failed at Hygiene. We have failed at Square Dancing. We have not been invited back to Improv. We have not been invited back to Taxidermy. We have not been invited back to Surgical Procedures 101. We have been whooped upside the head. We have been whipped into a frenzy. We have been told we lack initiative. We have been told we must learn to finish what we start. We might at one time have said, let's start a formal club, association, society, or religion. But of course, as we've been told, we lack follow-through. We have been told we take up too much space. We have been told that, at times, we appear to be in our own world. We have been told we need to stack the blocks in the corner neatly before we take our turn at the easel. We need to learn the skills of being invited back to formal clubs, associations, societies or religions. We need to learn the skills of judging distances. For example, distance can be judged by sound. If we see a gun fired in the distance, we can count the number of seconds between the flash and the sound of the explosion reaching us. In this way we can tell how far away we are from danger. If we see a gun fired close up, judging the distance will not be necessary and won't help us anyway. We have been told these are good skills to learn if we wish to make a solid contribution. We will learn the skills of basic survival. We will learn to tuck and roll. We will learn to make ourselves invisible.

Kathy Fish has been published in *Ploughshares*, *Washington Square Review*, *Denver Quarterly*, *Guernica*, *Best American Nonrequired Reading*, and elsewhere. Her work has appeared in three Norton anthologies of flash fiction as well as the *Norton Reader*. Honors include a Ragdale Foundation Fellowship and the Copper Nickel Editors' Prize.

TO YOU WHEN YOU'RE TWELVE AND YOU HATE YOURSELF:

ERICA FREDERICK

There are things that only people who really love you will tell you. Like, quiet as it's kept, most of your headspace will be taken up by a seventh-grade field trip, one in mid-May to Water Mania, where all the young ladies will have to wear the same red swimsuit, but only yours will be the one with very pubescent pubic hair seeping out the sides, spirals pushing against the spandex. Everyone will see, will jab their boy friends in the ribs to *holy shit, look look look*. You'll wonder what, you'll ask, *What?* And no one will tell you, because you should have known, you should have known how humiliating it is to have a body.

That's it, kid. In the end, the bush creeps down your thighs and up to underneath your navel. In some years, your skin will seethe, split into stretch marks, bright red on black skin because you keep becoming more you, bigger and more buoyant. Then you're twenty-six with a discerner's spirit, you've mostly forgiven yourself for not being all the way beautiful, and yet, you still wonder silly things, like if people see you as ridiculous but just won't say so. What if seventh graders are the best type of people there are because at least they let you know everyone *does* see you, that you *are* real. You wonder if you'll ever know anyone who loves you enough to tell you.

Love you to bits and pieces, and maybe back together again.

Erica Frederick is a queer, Haitian-American writer and MFA candidate in fiction at Syracuse University. She is the Fiction Coordinator for *The Best of the Net Anthology* and a Lambda Literary Fellow. You can find her tweeting into the void @ ericafrederick.

MY MOTHER'S DRESS SHOP

JEFF FRIEDMAN

Break down the boxes that held the clothing and stuff them into the dumpster in the alley behind the shop. Break down the racks that held the sexy dresses, the leather coats, the French lingerie until they are just rods and wheels lying in a corner. Fold up the clothing neatly. Break down the counter, the shelves, and the cash register empty of cash. Break down the shadows that no longer hold voices. Break down the light that drops through the window like a message until it is just a scrap of light. Break down the dust that clings to the walls and counters that your mother attacks with a cloth and Windex. Break down the mannikins until they are disconnected limbs, head, and torso. Now there is only the memory of a memory, the striped cat leaping on the counter, its tail ticking back and forth, the nurses in white uniforms peeking in the windows of air to spot a skirt or blouse on sale, your mother's voice coming back to you like the smells of a fresh cinnamon sweet roll and steaming black coffee, and the blaze of sun that makes it impossible to see.

Jeff Friedman has published nine collections of poetry and prose, including *The Marksman*, *Floating Tales*, and *Pretenders*. His tenth book, *Ashes in Paradise*, a collection of fabulist micro-fiction and prose poetry, is scheduled for publication by Madhat Press in spring 2023.

KAROL'S CLEANERS WILL CLEAN ANYTHING

JAMES R. GAPINSKI

That's what the sign says. When asked, Karol confirms, "Yes, anything. Read the sign, dipshit."

I normally wash my veggies at home, but these greens need professional help. The kale is dirty and limp, the broccoli is buggy. I load the nearest machine and add off-brand detergent. I set the gigantic dial to *fruits/vegetables* and deposit quarters. After a thirty-minute cycle, the greens are clean, plump, and crispy.

Back home, I chop my cleaned veggies. I realize I'm surrounded by other dirty things. A blackened skillet, a permanently stained Tupperware, a blender with gunk stuck in every crevasse. I return to Karol's. I set the dial: *miscellaneous hard objects*. After forty-five minutes, each item shines anew.

I smile and laugh. "This is amazing," I exclaim to the woman next to me. She scowls and moves her body in front of her washer, trying to block my view. She's cleaning a stack of envelopes emblazoned with words like *Final Notice* and *Past Due*.

Karol lowers her newspaper and says, "Don't bother the other customers, dipshit. People could be washing their unmentionables."

"Sorry, I didn't realize."

"That's no excuse," Karol says. She mumbles something else—probably calls me a dipshit again.

I take my polished kitchenware home, and I scramble to find other washables. I pull down dusty curtains. I roll up my white rug with its deep wine stains. I grab muddied camping gear.

Toward the back of my coat closet, I stumble upon the box you gave me. I used to look inside regularly, but now I've almost forgotten what it contains. Mom's wedding ring. The poem she wrote Dad for their thirtieth. Her hospital bracelet. Lots of photographs, mostly of us kids. Mom was often behind the camera rather than in front of it—a family historian unable to catalogue herself. The photos are yellowing. They need cleaning.

I go back to Karol's Cleaners. Karol lowers her paper again, but she doesn't call me a dipshit. She sees the box in my trembling hands. "Remember, we clean everything," she says. Her voice is gentle.

I set the dial to my name and climb into the washing machine. The drum aches under my weight, but it begins to spin. Water gushes. Thick foam rises.

James R. Gapinski (they/them) is the author of the novella *Edge of the Known Bus Line*. They are also the author of three fiction chapbooks, most recently *The Last Dinosaurs of Portland*. Learn more about their work at http://jamesrgapinski.com.

21 ALLEN DRIVE

DIANE GOTTLIEB

The way the deer gathered at dusk. The way the kids lay still on the trampoline, counting stars. The way the tall, thin pines stood so close their roots touched. The crisp night snows of November.

The Have-A-Hart traps for field mice seeking shelter in our home. The wide, sweeping windows, facing the woods. The vines and robins our painter stenciled on the dining room walls. The rooster he painted onto the kitchen table. Eggshell blue cabinets, butcher block counters, hickory boards underfoot.

I can still hear the tapping of woodpeckers, the yelps of wild turkeys as they charged our fearless terrier. I remember the soft tiny bat who made her home on our windowsill. The howling coyotes, alerting their pack of a kill.

The way my throat closed when I turned onto our long country driveway. The lights had not been turned on. The way my heart pounded when I opened the garage door to the empty spot where his Honda should have been. The way the house let us know. It was dark and silent, save the answering machine, screaming out flashes of red.

Diane Gottlieb writes nonfiction, and fiction—all of it true. She is the editor of *Awakenings: Stories of Body & Consciousness* (ELJ Editions 2023) and the Prose/CNF Editor of *Emerge Literary Journal*. You can find her at https://dianegottlieb.com and on Twitter @DianeGotAuthor.

24 HOUR ELEVATOR

RYAN GRIFFITH

To break down is what we're designed for. Lungs, language, elevators. A person can only climb seven floors before they grow old, before extinction, and it's me they call. Shaman, doctor, repair man. An elevator is a machine of vertical desire, weight and balance, worm wheels and the overdrive governor, and never relents. Day and night it slips invisible through walls, silent as germs, drawing us closer to our tribe of shadows. As sometimes happens with the heart, things go wrong, and the tiny capsule hangs in the void, pinched between floors. Tonight it's a single woman stranded in the infinite divisibility of space, the impossibility of arrival. What is she doing all alone in that steel box? Like us, she listens to the clock of the world, unnecklaces the jewels of memory. Wait for me, my angel. We are more than our nervous systems, hot breath on glass. If you speak to darkness it will answer: *I am the spoon of suffering, the cup of sand we drink.* The night is genius, beautiful as smoke. Palmists in their mystic kitchens touch the red eyes of cigarettes to the sky. I see you dangling in the shaft, my dear. Don't worry. We all need our myths of free fall, that there is no safety brake, that we drop screaming through the beast. You only think you want the doors to open. It's hard to return to this world once you say goodbye.

Ryan Griffith's fiction has appeared in *The Ekphrastic Review*, *Flash Boulevard*, *New World Writing Quarterly*, *The Wigleaf Top 50 Very Short Stories of 2012* and *2022*, and elsewhere. He runs a multimedia narrative installation in San Diego called *Relics of the Hypnotist War*. Visit his website at relicsofthe-hypnotistwar.com.

THE EXTINCTION MUSEUM: EXHIBIT #506 (HOME PREGNANCY TEST, C. EARLY 2000S)

TINA MAY HALL

That spider had to die. I knew it was bad luck, but it was the size of a knuckle, deep in slumber, until it wasn't, scrabbling all around the corner of the back door. After killing it, I drank the last of the tequila to calm down, and then the bad shit started. All the spider ladies from my nightmares crowded into the room, mandibles clacking, hats askew, webbed mouths spitting muffled opera. I didn't much like it, but could have lived with their uneasy company. But then the millipede hauled itself up out of the basement, where the water stood ready for electrocuting and where all my unfertilized eggs sank. In my youth, it was scorpions we feared. And sewer cockroaches hard as baseballs, thwacking my head in the park at night, where I went to kiss my first love, and feel skin on my skin until the car battery died and the palmetto bugs drawn to the headlights found their way inside. Was there any escaping the despair of those sectioned bodies, persistent as dirty laundry, crusted dishes, menstrual blood, and those damn scuff marks on the terracotta tile that was shipped from Spain in boxes infested with silverfish? So many small exorcisms, each one a snuff of the soul, tiny flame of a life crushed by my own flesh.

Tina May Hall is the author of *The Physics of Imaginary Objects* and *The Snow Collectors*. Her work has appeared in *SmokeLong Quarterly*, *Wigleaf*, *Big Other*, *Quarterly West*, *Black Warrior Review*, *The Collagist*, and other journals.

WHAT WE BELIEVED

D.E. HARDY

Art class was the best hour of the week; Miss
Cunningham's poster of the color wheel told the
truth—everything had an opposite—blue to yellow,
green to red; our desks were magic shields; sharpened
pencils smelled like progress; Billy Sullivan was a
genius because he knew things like England just got
the bomb, and Brad Majors was right when he said
the Russians were gonna get it—it was two against
one now; owning a television meant you mattered;
recess was never long enough; math was boring;
Janey Vanderpelt smelled because she had cooties;
lunch revealed worth, like how Micky Lane's mom
gave him store-bought pastries, the good kind from
the commercials, or the opposite, how Lena Smitty
always ate even the core of her apple; communism was
a dirty word; the way a green crayon glided across
craft paper felt clean as new money; Superman chose
America for a reason; gum stayed in your stomach
until you died; it was comforting how we all drew
the same landscape, a good omen, the same green
field, wide and unencumbered, the same tall, blue
sky; God loved Americans more than other people,

so maybe it wouldn't hurt when it happened—the blast—maybe it would just be a piercing light that turned the world its opposite for a moment, a sky of gold and a red earth, maybe we could peek out from under our desks to see the brilliance, a long white horizon, outstretched like arms, beckoning us home.

D.E. Hardy's work has appeared in *Pithead Chapel*, *X-R-A-Y Literary Magazine*, *Lost Balloon*, *FlashBack Fiction*, *New World Writing Quarterly*, among others. She lives in the San Francisco Bay Area.

WHEN YOU'RE THE CONTORTIONIST

CANDACE HARTSUYKER

It happens like this: your sister is skipping with a jump rope, her feet *slap slapping* the sidewalk. You go into the house to get a glass of water, and when you come back, your sister, her sneakers that are bright as Wite-Out, and her sparkly pink jump rope are gone.

After her disappearance, your father's restless hands will hold a length of rope: he'll tie and untie it, reconstruct the sailor's knots he learned when he was a boy. The figure eight, the bowline, the clove hitch.

You will deal with your grief by tying yourself into an intricate pattern of knots. You'll step onto the living room coffee table and slowly go into a backbend. It will remind you of the game of Twister you played at parties, a foot sliding backwards and to the right, a leg crossing under someone else's arm. Your feet will move toward your hands until you are grasping your ankles. Your head will move back until only your throat is exposed. Then, you'll stand back up.

Next, you'll drag your father's suitcase from out of the hall closet, twist and bend, contort your body into its smallest shape. You'll move as gracefully as a Slinky that is being cradled from one hand to the other. Once you are safely inside, you'll close your eyes and pretend the suitcase is partly zipped up, leaving a small pocket of air so you can breathe. You'll practice twisting your body into smaller and smaller knots until you are a balled-up knot that can't be untied.

You'll spend nights imagining your sister being picked up from the patch of sidewalk, then thrown into the trunk of a car. You'll fold yourself into a myriad of animal shapes: a frog, a swan, a wolf. You'll imagine what it is like to be kidnapped. On the days you are the saddest, you will tangle your limbs until your body is not flesh but rough and fibrous, a snarl of grief, a human knot. You'll practice becoming a girl who can squeeze into spaces smaller than a fist.

One day, you'll arch your arms over your head and turn your body into the shape of a key. You'll find your sister behind a locked door. She'll be there, waiting.

Candace Hartsuyker has an MFA in Creative Writing from McNeese State University. Her work has been published in *Fiction Southeast*, *CHEAP POP* and *Okay Donkey Magazine*.

THE DEATHS OF THE GREAT LAKES

JEFFREY HERMANN

THE DEATH OF LAKE MICHIGAN

First we took one last, long swim. Someone fished and yelled when he pulled up a walleye. I was given the honor of turning up the sun. God, the heat! By shading our eyes we could see it all turn to vapor. We were packing up towels and folding chairs when the fisherman approached me.

"Take this fish," he told me.

"Take this fish," he begged.

"Take it."

THE DEATH OF LAKE ERIE

We led a giant to the edge of the lake. The ground shook with his walloping stomps. His giant daughter walked beside him, holding his big hand. Using a sewer pipe like a straw, he sucked and drank until it was dry. The lakebed was like an endless barren planet. The giant's daughter was the only one who cried. And this you won't believe: A woman found the necklace she'd lost as a child, there in the stinking mud. When the giant told the story to his girl, she opened her mouth in awe.

THE DEATH OF LAKE ONTARIO

We kicked it full of sand and lawn clippings, boxes, clothes, bricks—anything we could drag over there. On top of that we built a beautiful pretend lake. It was made of tinted glass. Children were allowed to draw fish and beavers and boats on the panes. One made a mistake and drew a giraffe. Some people complained, saying it was unrealistic. I liked it. I liked how it seemed happy down there, not realizing it needed air. I liked that it was smiling.

THE DEATH OF LAKE SUPERIOR

It hung itself.

THE DEATH OF LAKE HURON

Some men came offering to buy it, but they only wanted the liquid, nothing living or dead in there. We filtered everything out the best we could. After the men hauled it all away we found the souls of everyone who had ever drowned. They wanted to go back to their old lives now—school children, wives, hotel managers, etc. We said it can't work like that. They sank back into the sand and rocks, their appa-

ritions like a thick, gray muck. That was surprising.
All this time we'd dreamed them a watery blue.

Jeffrey Hermann's poetry and prose has appeared in *Okay Donkey Magazine*, *Heavy Feather Review*, *Passages North*, *trampset*, and other publications. Though less publicized, he finds his work as a father and husband to be rewarding beyond measure.

POTENTIAL

SABRINA HICKS

When I was in junior high, I took up palm reading. I wanted to know what the world had in store for me and everyone I came in contact with. I bought books, watched YouTube videos, sketched diagrams into the night, then I'd reach for the soft hands of my classmates before the bell rang, trace the lines in their palms with my finger and say things like: *you will have a long life; you will get married at twenty-eight; you will come into money, but only briefly because you divorce three times you whore, ha-ha.*

Sometimes I'd spin long and sordid tales, but I knew the lengths and intersections of the lines, the direction of their meaning—though I never let the truth get in the way. And the kids would line up like I knew things, like I had answers. I was a fraud, of course, because I believed in potential over fate. Fate had only given me a small life, in a small town, and I was determined to take over, widen my circle, make my own fate, thinking all my friendships and love interests were most likely ones born out of convenience, proximity, comfort.

I could find an excuse to pick up the inky hand of the poet in my English class, two rows away, a boy who wrote dark poems in his notebook, on every side margin, no white space to be had, words soaring off the page onto his skin. A boy who by the end of our high school years, would drive to a big city, find a bridge, and jump. I held his hand, saw the shortness of his lines, the crazy dissections, the fractured groves marking past trauma. I wanted to take his pen and redraw the lines into wings. *What?* he said. *No good?* I slowly traced the broken bits like I was trying to connect and repair them. Then I put my palm on top of his and told him I saw potential. *So much fucking potential.*

Sabrina Hicks' work has appeared in numerous journals, *Best Small Fictions*, *Best Microfiction*, and *Wigleaf's Top 50*. She most recently won the Cleaver and Five South Journal Flash Fiction contests. More of her stories can be found at sabrinahicks.com.

WHEN THE COWBOY SEPARATES THE CALVES FOR TOMORROW'S BRANDING—

SABRINA HICKS

—the mothers will bawl in the pastures, their babies will huddle together in the pens, the cowboy will remember his mother leaving, his daddy whipping him for being inconsolable.

When the cowboy separates the calves for tomorrow's branding, the cowboy's wife knows he will drink too much whiskey, will cry out in his sleep, will wake to the bawling outside their window, pull a pillow over his head, say, *I'm going to whip their hide.*

When the cowboy separates the calves for tomorrow's branding, the cowboy will learn he'll become a father, later learn it's a son, later learn his cries, later learn he himself is haunted.

But for now, babies by their sides, the cows are quiet and content, heads buried in the thick sweetgrass; and the cowboy and his wife wake to birdsong, wake in an embrace, wake with a sliver of sunlight stretching across their quilted bed.

Sabrina Hicks' work has appeared in numerous journals, *Best Small Fictions*, *Best Microfiction*, and *Wigleaf's Top 50*. She most recently won the Cleaver and Five South Journal Flash Fiction contests. More of her stories can be found at sabrinahicks.com.

BREATH

BRUCE JOHNSON

Rodney and I believed if we held our breath too long we might die. We spent our afternoons up on his roof, taking turns. The roof faced nothing but a big tree, so no one ever saw. We'd time each other on the stopwatch I stole from school, and Rodney would always say something like, "If I get a minute thirty, you got to kiss my shoe." Or bet me: "More than two minutes, that means my mom's coming back."

My mom had told me not to play with Rodney after I stepped on an upturned nail in his dad's workshed. His hair was greasy and he smelled like talcum powder. Years later we'd lose touch after he fell hard into drugs. But Rodney had the lungs of a whale. He'd go a minute thirty at least, then his eyes would roll back in his head. I knew he was putting me on, but still, every time, I'd hunch over him in a panic, slapping color into his cheeks until he opened his eyes. He told me stories about the things he saw: tunnels of light, dead relatives in robes, animals assembled from spare car parts, women with forked tongues. "That was a close one," he'd say. "I almost didn't make it back." But he always did, and that was the point, at least back then. That there was nothing you couldn't come back from.

Bruce Johnson holds a PhD in Creative Writing & Literature from the University of Southern California. His stories have appeared in *Joyland*, *The Cincinnati Review MiCRo Series*, *The Los Angeles Review*, *Adroit*, and elsewhere. He lives with his wife and son in Santiago, Chile, and can be found at bruce-johnsonfiction.com.

A FIELD GUIDE TO PREHISTORIC MOTHERHOOD

SHELLY JONES

Mark off a quadrant along the rocky shelf with string and wooden stakes to demarcate your nest. This is where you will sit for hours, knees bent, as you methodically scrape a centimeter of dirt away with a worn trowel, uncovering what's hidden beneath. Tap carefully with a metal pick, detecting the tonal differences between rock, bone, clay: a paleontologist's favorite tune.

With each new discovery, catalog the fossils: teeth, vertebrae, all preserved by strata of the earth like a mother's arms.

As the hours wear on, use a brush of sable to gingerly expose the fragile shell, thinner than bone, stronger than muscle. Marvel at its perfection, everything intact for millennia.

The egg measures seven inches, the same length as the small coffin you once buried in similar sandstone soil, a crumpled sonogram and dinosaur-themed onesie sharing the shallow plot. You're surprised by how little it weighs, less than a human child, and yet how enormous it could become.

That night, you sleep fitfully in your cot. Wind whips across the barren landscape; dust eddies, knocking on your canvas tent. Shivering, you'll think of the skeletal egg, exposed, alone, in the dinosaur graveyard.

Step gingerly into the excavation site. Be careful not to disturb the fossils. Curl your body concave around the egg, your stomach pressed firmly against the shell. Let your heat incubate the embryo; wait patiently to hear the nearly imperceptible scritch of a scaly claw yearning to break free: a sound only a mother would know.

Shelly Jones (she/they) is a professor at a small college in upstate New York, where she teaches mythology, folklore, and writing. Her speculative work has been published by *The Magazine of Fantasy & Science Fiction*, *Apex Magazine*, *The Future Fire*, and more. Find them on Twitter @shellyjansen and https://shellyjonesphd.wordpress.com/.

GROCERIES

TUCKER LEIGHTY-PHILLIPS

I've been trying to keep to the outer perimeter of the grocery store. Health websites say it's the best way to avoid processed foods. Most of the good stuff, milk and fresh produce, are along the border. Like a moat, or a barricade. Isn't that funny, all the good protecting the unsavory. Feels like a metaphor. To be honest, I stick to the outside because there's more space, less constriction moving around a table filled with peaches than, say, the cracker aisle. There is a sense of drowning among those center lanes. When I see a buggy at the end of one, I think of cage doors. Entrapment. The end of things. Which also makes me think of Jonah, you know, the guy from the whale, or, rather, the guy in the whale. I played him in a church production once. They asked me to do it because they could tell my faith was starting to teeter, cowering from the church bus when it pulled in the driveway, begging my mother to shoo it on from the window. They came back Monday morning, offered me the lead role. Jonah ends up inside the fish as a test of his faith, or something. That's how I felt, up on stage, in the center of a paper mâché whale, newspaper articles about high school softball games bleeding through the blue paint. The whale was waiting for my re-devotion. In the grocery store, fish can be found on the outer barrier, usually in the back. Salmon, tuna, maybe haddock, depending on region and time of year. Sometimes there's one of those lobster aquariums. When I was a kid, I thought the aquarium was a magnifying glass, and the lobsters were actually much smaller than they looked. Little palm-resting crustaceans. Practically crawdads. I'll never know where I got the idea. Maybe I wanted them to be tiny enough to escape without notice. Maybe, to me at least, being trapped in something massive made you small by default.

MR. BOGGINS

TUCKER LEIGHTY-PHILLIPS

There is a knock on the classroom door. Before Mr. Boggins can rise from his desk to answer, it opens. At the door is a police officer, and he beckons the teacher over. They step into the hallway, closing the door behind them. We look around, inspecting one another, silently beginning interrogations. Is it him, or is it one of us? We start thinking of the rumors we'd heard that week, the list of potential suspects. Someone said Josh Manensky had brought a magnet to the computer lab and dragged it across three towers, frying them all. An eighteen-year-old senior had gotten in a fight with a freshman and might be tried as an adult. We had all made salacious posts on message boards, which we'd heard the principal was monitoring. Maybe one of us had taken it too far. Or perhaps it was Boggins himself. A girl in the cafeteria said she'd seen him at Liquor Bonanza buying vodka, and that he was an alcoholic. Could Mr. Boggins be arrested for being an alcoholic? Could the girl in the cafeteria be arrested for spreading rumors? Could we be arrested for wanting Mr. Boggins to be the one getting arrested? William, the class clown, teetered towards the door and put an ear against the glass pane. *I can't hear anything*, he mouthed, but by then, they'd already heard him, and he was in the hallway too.

Tucker Leighty-Phillips is the author of *Maybe This Is What I Deserve* (Split/Lip Press 2023). He lives in Whitesburg, Kentucky. Find him online at TuckerLP.net.

9 DYSTOPIAS

MONICA LOUZON

I.

Sophia orders a fancy cheese knife on Amazon while she talks on the phone with David. It's misuse of corporate time, but the company has bigger fish to fry. The world's about to end. Delivery before curfew, arriving at 19:00h! Lockdown's at 19:30h.

II.

David's home, ordering books to read on the sly. He reviews his science fiction collection. He hesitates, then orders some audiovisual media Sophia won't like.

Why shouldn't he indulge?

He clears his browser history.

III.

David's an Uber driver taking an annoyingly chatty author to DC. He merges onto the Beltway when the radio orders them to immediately turn off all cell and navigation signals. He powers down his phone, turns off his GPS.

A mile later, people vault the Beltway's jersey walls, run out into the chaos and dodge cars.

David's not sure what they're running from.

The author cheerfully says the infection's spreading.

IV.

A team of analysts studies metadata, tries to identify patterns. Every time the author travels, a new outbreak starts.

There's something else in the metadata too: She's not from here.

V.

The Visitors turn a highway in LA into a rotating Möbius strip in midair. Humanity surrenders. The Visitors teach humans how to tap the highway for energy—an electromagnetic windmill. They teach humanity how to build.

VI.

David watches from the highway, proud father of a human daughter and a ship. His baby, the USS *Something*, hovers over LA at a forty-five degree angle—bow-first. Once boarding and cabin check are complete, this ark will leave Earth with its fake sails. Gotta maintain that Hollywood aesthetic.

VII.

Sophia grabs her favorite spatula—for eggs, and pancakes of nostalgia. She tries to stay calm while her two younger kids each fill their own pillowcases.

David's got her firstborn, Emma. No time to find him. Her lover's at the spaceport, waiting.

VIII.

David's on the USS *Something*. Emma can't come. Sophia didn't give permission. It'd be kidnapping. Suit Man can't help—Sophia's in the USS *Something's* corporate government, and some high-ranking official's in her.

Everyone aboard wears jumpsuits and indentured servitude—except for Suit Man.

Suit Man doesn't want to risk crossing Sophia. Imagine the fallout.

IX.

Emma's in a cornfield.

The cop car's still running. They shout threats. Their beams reflect off hungry eyes.

Emma swallows her tears and fears. The eyes pounce.

She presses the pedal, fishtailing.

Monica Louzon (she/her) is a queer Maryland writer, translator, and editor. Her words have appeared in *Apex Magazine*, *After the Storm*, *Constelación Magazine*, *Paranoid Tree Press*, *Shoreline of Infinity*, and others. She is Acquiring Editor for *The Dread Machine*.

SNAPPER

NICHOLAS MAINIERI

They tie to the platform down current so the Gulf won't pull them into the machinery. The unmanned rig shrieks on a timer, its peal pressing into the boy's brain, squeezing out all else; his father explains that this is to alert tankers to the platform's presence in low visibility.

"Has to be loud enough for that."

The sound rings in the boy's eardrums and then fades.

The mooring rope creaks, taut across the gunwale.

His father's reel clicks.

The boy watches for sea turtles because he has a book about them at his mother's. Greens and leatherbacks and loggerheads and hawksbills. He'll know which on sight.

The rig shrieks again.

Countless other scaffolds bristle gray on the horizon. All of them out there screaming.

They must be.

Nor had the boy foreseen how a red snapper's

stomach would swell and bulge from its mouth once they got it into the boat. It makes his own stomach feel the same, like he might puke.

"They in that cold deep water," his father says. "Pull 'em up too fast and it's like scuba divers with the air bubbles in their blood—you know what I'm talking about?"

No, the boy doesn't. Not that. What he sees instead is how there's a world above you. How maybe there's always a world above you. Worlds upon worlds, each as real as anything. Separate worlds, each there without you. They don't need you, and they don't need you to know. But then you do, lip on a hook. Next world up. Can't work the other way. Next world. It's yours now, too.

Nicholas Mainieri is the author of *The Infinite*, a novel. His short stories and essays have appeared in publications including *The Southern Review*, *The Cincinnati Review*, *Longreads*, *The Southern Humanities Review*, and *Notre Dame Magazine*, among others. He holds an MFA from the University of New Orleans.

CURE FOR TEARS

AVRA MARGARITI

He has black eyes (red in the dark) (he makes love with his eyes closed always). Tears flooding his waterlines—a common phenomenon. They bloat all his secondhand books; his lush houseplants wither under salt. The coarse plates of his scaly skin eat through tissues and embroidered handkerchiefs, quick as a kiss.

Corduroy jacket, dark jeans, sneakers wrapped in brown tape because his claws grow faster than he can trim them. *He's so fake,* friends of a friend whisper to each other in the street. *Crocodile cry-baby.*

In a support group for empaths, a young man sat across from him winks and a crystalline tear rolls down a smooth cheek. They go home together afterward, where they cry each other lakes, rivers, and other bodies. The downstairs neighbors write complaint letters about the water staining their ceiling.

Next there is a girl, her touch gentle like a butterfly landing on his snout. She says she doesn't get sad, not anymore. True enough, his eyes dehydrate whenever he's with her. He entertains the idea that she's his cure, but he can't overlook the blankness of her gaze. The wool-sweater-itchiness of his eyeballs gets old fast, anyway. She sticks a lit cigarette between his sharp front teeth, and he resolves to save up for tear duct removal surgery.

He has black eyes (red from secondhand grief) (eyelids always closed if he can help it) (the tears still squeeze through).

They all leave eventually, salt deposits on his unmade bed, unopened letters detailing the long existence of pain followed by the brief absence of it, and thank you, lover, for helping me carry this weight of mine, if only for a little bit.

See you later (alligator). After a while (crocodile). Xx

Avra Margariti is a queer author and poet from Greece. Avra's work haunts publications such as *Wigleaf*, *SmokeLong Quarterly*, *Best Microfiction*, and *Best Small Fictions*. You can find Avra on Twitter (@avramargariti).

GREASE AND FEATHERS

LEILA MARTIN

I feed Dead Bird popcorn. She rustles up to the pile; a scruffy dart, dark against my blanket. She pecks, but it falls right through her. I wipe grease on my jeans, wonder when they last got washed. I turn down the TV. I should go to sleep. She cocks her head, watches me with eyes the colour of milk. I wish she'd blink.

Dead Bird walks with me home from school, her crooked shoulders creaking. She glints in the sun like scribbled graphite. We pass the paving where I first found her, splayed moth-flat and waiting. We turn onto my street; my gut shrivels. She stares. Extends a smelly wing.

I pocket my key and click the door closed. Press my brow to the wood. The tide of tempers already rising from the kitchen. We soft-tread the stairs, just to be safe. I turn up the TV. I hate canned laughter. So fake. I make it louder. The sun sinks. I turn off the TV to a new, leaden silence.

Dead Bird tap-dances at the window, skittish as shredded paper. So I take her to the skate park.

Conifers bristle into the dusk. Concrete yawns an invite and I ignore the grit in my sneaker, taste the dry waves of cig smoke and follow the fireflies. Roll and scrape and scrape and roll again; our future spans wild, somewhere else, if we can get there fast enough. She wants to fly. And who am I to stop her?

Leila Martin is a freelance writer from the UK, where she shares a small house with a small number of people and a tremendous number of books. Her stories have appeared in *Fireside Magazine*, *Cossmass Infinities* and *Daily Science Fiction*. You can find her on Twitter @Bookishleels.

WORKSHOP

KATHLEEN MCGOOKEY

Once I offered a poem that contained the phrase "mist shimmers" to a table full of people. One man said, *Mist can't shimmer. Fog shimmers. Mist drifts.* His name was Paul. I said nothing but thought many things. Paul had dark bangs cut straight across his forehead, clean fingernails, and a cardigan that smelled like charcoal briquets. He sliced an apple right on top of the growing sheaf of poems, and he didn't share. He counted the rings of the apple's life. Paul said crows didn't live in Antarctica, because they couldn't cross the ocean. He seemed to know a lot about weather and birds, but little about wishbones and the kind of moss that sprouts tendrils wearing tiny triangular hats. The ringing in my ears shifted from side to side, then grew louder and faded, like some kid was playing with the controls offstage. I don't remember what Paul's poem was about.

Kathleen McGookey's most recent book is *Instructions for My Imposter* (Press 53). Her work has appeared in journals including *Copper Nickel*, *December*, *Field*, *Glassworks*, *Miramar*, *Ploughshares*, *Prairie Schooner*, *Quiddity*, and *Sweet*. She has received grants from the French Ministry of Foreign Affairs and the Sustainable Arts Foundation.

TUSKS

ROSS MCMEEKIN

One day we all grew tusks, one pointing out from each cheek. Surprisingly few accommodations needed to be made. Motorcycle helmets, scuba gear—any solid thing wrapped around the face no longer worked. But other than that, we got used to them. Sleep was not a problem because no one really ever sleeps facedown. Blowing one's nose was difficult, and kissing was shot, but eating was okay.

Soon we began to enjoy the tusks. We shined and buffed them. We illustrated and tagged them. We etched the names of our loved ones through the enamel. We carved religious texts and memorials and celebrity profiles into the dentine. We invented outfits for them, for when we went out to the office, parties, and so on. Soon we imagined our ancestors having them. Then we imagined aliens having them. Finally, we imagined God having them. It was then that we all made a pact and cut them off. It was then that we grew tails.

Ross McMeekin is author of a noir, *The Hummingbirds*. His stories have appeared in places such as *Virginia Quarterly Review*, *Shenandoah*, and *Cease, Cows*. He edits the literary journal *Spartan* and lives with his wife and family north of Seattle.

THE KNIFE THROWER'S DAUGHTER

FRANKIE MCMILLAN

1

When your mama's a knife thrower you know the meaning of perfection. It's not good enough for her to try her best or come close, she has to be 100 percent on the mark so that when those knives come hurtling towards you they land around you, not inside you. You know it's possible, a life without error, but you also know, and this is what you learn from your papa, that there is always a way to escape, to escape from the humdrum of routine, of rehearsals, of always being perfect.

2

You're standing there against the back of the rehearsal tent, the smell of last night's curry in the air, your mama steadying herself, head bent. She faces you, picks up a knife. Her tattooed arm draws back and it's right then, you can't help it, this wayward thought . . . what if you were to twitch just a little bit, and you feel the niggly twitch in your shoulders, you can't stop the terrible thought, the way people do, who suddenly feel an urge to throw their babies off bridges, or leap in front of an incoming train, or pick up a gun and pull the trigger.

3

Your mama looks at you intently, your mama can see inside you, all your dark thoughts. She knows you secretly see your papa in town. She knows you'd rather live with him. Your mama drops the knife. She steps over the trapeze wires towards you. It could be she screams in your face. *Do you want to get yourself killed!* Or it could be she puts her arms around you.

Either way, you know it's going to be perfect.

Frankie McMillan is a poet and short fiction writer from Aotearoa New Zealand. Her latest book, *The Wandering Nature of Us Girls* (Canterbury University Press), was published in 2022.

WHAT BONES CARRY

JANNA MILLER

The mathematician's skeleton propped in the corner of the anatomy and physiology room, not far from where he used to teach. Strung together with wire and metal pins. Sometimes he was used for instruction, though mostly he held feather boas and Mardi Gras beads. One semester he wore a wide-brimmed sun hat, someone's lost and never found.

Equations slipped away, into a permanent bone density. The skeleton remembered one, about orbital distance, though that had less to do with his eye sockets and more to do with planets. In the quiet of calcium space, it didn't seem an important distinction. It was all space, they were all planets.

Flesh and blood talked and talked. He jiggled with the movement of their mouths. The springs on his jaw bounced his teeth into each other, clattering old fillings. Low whispers matched their thrumming heartbeats and sharp breaths. He felt outward through his ribcage, absorbing vibrations through calcaneus and phalanges.

Two hooks held the hemispheres of his skull

together. Unhinged, his rough bone bowl hid love notes, broken pencils, and a piece of mint gum stuck to his petrous ridge. One diamond cufflink had been embedded soon after he was pieced and delivered—drilled and covered with putty. At the last, a kiss landed with no vibration at all. The skeleton did not remember why.

Memory did not store in bones, but leached out with the soft tissue, light as breath. Marrow held strength and silence. Persistence and endurance. Now that he was stripped of all else, the mathematician's skeleton aligned with granite and sediment and quartz. His contents kept out of time. Not a thought, but a truth. All bones carry it.

Librarian, mother, and minor trickster, Janna has published in *SmokeLong Quarterly*, CHEAP POP, *Whale Road Review*, *Necessary Fiction*, *The Citron Review*, and others. Her story collection, *All Lovers Burn at the End of the World* is forthcoming from SLJ Editions in 2024. Generally, if the toaster blows up, it is not her fault.

CENTAURS IN THE LAUNDROMAT

LYNN MUNDELL

It's midnight at the Double Bubble and I've finally made it to the spin cycle. Now that the eleven loads are clean, they are transformed from a monumental failure in hygiene to an accomplishment. In a corner the attendant is leaning against a counter reading a waterlogged copy of Dante's *Inferno* while a fly bothers his chestnut rump and legs. I'd heard the centaur was close to retirement. Earlier he'd emptied his leather saddlebag of T-shirts and blankets into the three remaining washers, horseshoes clattering against the tile floor. I watch my clothes chase each other's tails and think I'm probably too old to wear zebra print bras, while from a speaker The Shirelles sing about still loving me tomorrow. Hey, I say to the centaur. Without looking up, he says, Hay is for horses. I'd heard he was aloof. I try again. So, they're putting you out to pasture soon. Now he does look at me, dark eyes sparkling in anger, mane of greying hair bristling, one earlobe heavy with a dull gold hoop, and I remember he's also been described as aggressive. Sorry, poor choice of words, I say, and he returns to his reading. Just us, the machines, two slow clocks, and walls of glass. Outside the darkness stares in. I've never been good with men or horses. Too forward with one; too backward with the other. Is it too late? One by one, the washers all quit. Quiet like an audience before a performance begins. The centaur has become lost in the story. I lift armfuls of our damp laundry— my camisoles and leg warmers; his knit vests and bandanas—and amble to the dryers, stuffing them full and then feeding each from a bag of old silver coins. The buckles from the horse blankets ping musically. When "Unchained Melody" starts, I hum along, remembering, remembering. Now the centaur is beside me, humming too. He smells of Old Spice and barn. He lifts my arms up round his neck, where my batwing fat sways just a bit. And then his own weathered limbs tighten around my thickening middle. Slowly we manage an old school box step with our eight legs. Outside the night has lost interest in us and is moving on to the future, while within the bright laundromat our closest intimates dance and buck.

CHILTEPIN

LYNN MUNDELL

When Uncle gives you the hottest pepper from his collection of potted chilis, he doesn't see a pepper. He sees the tiny crimson circle of the faraway Japanese flag during the Battle of Iwo Jima when he was nineteen.

When you accept the pepper from Uncle, you don't see a pepper. You see a strawberry Jujube, a red chocolate Sixlet, a cherry Dot. You see the movie concession stand, feel the big velvet seats, hear the kids all singing "Everybody Wants to Be a Cat."

When the fieriest pepper in the solar system enters your mouth, it isn't a fruit or a candy. It is Venus, the planet that melts metal. Evaporates water. Suffocates. The one completely foreign to Earth, its closest neighbor.

When Uncle looks at you, he sees you're screaming like you've been shot. He sees the discarded pepper like a drop of blood in the dirt. When you look at Uncle, you see someone with a garden of weapons. You see an enemy posing as an ally.

Lynn Mundell's writing has appeared in *The Masters Review*, *Booth*, and *SmokeLong Quarterly*, and been honored with the Lascaux Prize in Creative Nonfiction. Her fiction chapbook is *Let Our Bodies Be Returned to Us* (Yemassee, University of South Carolina). Lynn is the editor of the literary journal *Centaur*.

WINDOWS

ELIZABETH MARIA NARANJO

We wait until the soft explosions above deaden to absolute silence—not the kind of silence that listens but the kind that sleeps, and teenage girls know the difference. We wait until our murmurs turn to whispers and even the whispers seem loud—muffled collisions, muted giggles. Fingers fumbling at the silver latch of a basement window. We crawl through the narrow opening, climb over the well, roll onto cold grass. Streak across the backyard and scale the fence like wood sprites, two girls—jeans, sweaters, sneakers, cigarettes. We run.

Dark empty streets, a world asleep, the gift of midnight. Our voices now like bells. We light our cigarettes and inhale deeply, listening to the paper crackle, watching the embers momentarily glow brighter before they turn to ash. We blow jets of smoke into the night air. We have nowhere to go, and nowhere is enough.

Another night, another bedroom, this one aboveground. We slide the window open, quietly, carefully, pop the screen. We lower ourselves gently onto the gravel, tiptoe across the gravel, wince at the comically amplified sound of our sneakers on the gravel. We leap silent onto the gray strip of sidewalk and bound across the street, waving at the neighborhood boy who sits on his front porch smoking, friendly face, long blonde hair—he waves back. Later we will stop for boys, later boys will run with us, after us, they will pick us up in cars and drive us places and buy us alcohol. But for now it's just us.

Maybe we'll walk to the elementary school and climb the highest horizontal bars—one with chipped blue paint, one with chipped yellow paint—eight feet up, sitting, falling, coordinating death drops so our feet hit the ground at the exact same time.

Maybe we'll jump onto the swings, side by side, long brown hair streaming, voices shrieking, kicking our legs higher and higher until our feet shatter the moon.

Elizabeth Maria Naranjo is a writer in Tempe, Arizona. Her work has appeared in *Brevity Magazine*, *Superstition Review*, *Fractured Lit*, *The Portland Review*, *Reservoir Road*, *Hunger Mountain*, and a few other places. Elizabeth's work has been nominated for the Pushcart Prize, Best American Essay, and Best of the Net.

HER MOTHER, MY MOTHER

HEMA NATARAJU

Her mother never wore a sari, my mother never did not. Her mother drove a Mustang, my mother walked everywhere, even though I hated being picked up last. Her mother never packed her lunches, my mother packed feasts, though I wanted greasy, stale pizza from the cafeteria like everyone else. Her mother allowed sleepovers, my mother trusted no one, not even friends. Her mother went on business trips, my mother was . . . my mother, nothing else.

Some nights I wished I could swap my mother for hers. She looked skywards at planes growing smaller and smaller, and wished the same.

Hema Nataraju is an Indian-American writer and mom, currently based in Singapore. Her work has most recently appeared in *Five South, Booth, Wigleaf, 100 Word Story, Ruby Literary*, and *Nurture Literary*, among others. She is a Submissions Editor at *SmokeLong Quarterly* and she tweets as m_ixedbag.

THE FOX

BISHOP V. NAVARRO

On your deathbed, you smell like that night. That convenience store and how we swam in its green-sweet fluorescence to buy up cream sodas. We covered our faces against the gas fumes as I pumped and you stood staring down the quiet highway. We needed the tank full enough to get us to the edge of town where the other locals said a dog-man haunted that brambled field. We got there and hopped the thin fence hugging it. I wanted to find the dog-man and tell him everything would be okay.

Who we actually found was Jesus Christ, sweeping his palm over the ground in front of him. Light emanated. He had lost his pet fox. She must have dug under the pearly gates, snuck past St. Peter, and dove down some portal. Her name was Tabitha and she'd been gone for three days. Jesus wept.

We split up from Him to help search and after the heat sweat through my shirt, I spotted her rolling in the grass, chattering. She was okay. You carried her while we found Jesus and then passed her off to Him like she was a baby that fell asleep on the drive home. They ascended and you and I waved.

In the hospital, I hear a breeze pass from the hallway, through the door, over your body. Now you smell like red wine. You lift your arms, and then they drop.

Bishop V. Navarro (they/she) is a poet, fiction writer, and media critic living in Tampa, FL. She holds an MFA from the University of South Florida where she currently pursues a PhD in Communication.

AVAILABLE IN STANDARD SIZES

CHRISTOPHER NOTARNICOLA

They press to your chest a half-jacket—just the part of the dress uniform that the camera needs to convince your friends and family of your newfound commitment to country—the front. You stand in line with the unphotographed. They call you without your name. They focus on your image. Look this way, they say, and they dare you to smile. You do not smile. They take the picture and take back the half-jacket before the flash haze fades. Your mother will keep a two-by-three in the visor of her car for the eight months you spend overseas. Her mother will pin a four-by-six to the prayer board in the vestibule of her church where it will collect blessings long after your return. They will say you take a handsome picture. How strange, this centering of attentions. They will praise your development from a curious child into this—this marine in their hands—so you will thank them, and they will lower their chins and lift their smiles and insist. No, they'll say, thank you. You struggle to refocus your vision. They hang the half-jacket and shove you off and call for the next in line. You stand in line with the photographed.

One in front turns to ask if you think there will be more pictures or if the one is all. You imagine one is all, whisper one is all, but you tell yourself there will be more, at least as many as have come before, and you think back to the point-and-shoot camera in the backseat of your truck, pixels waiting in the dark like a future, like your four-by-six past cross-sectioned in a stack at the bottom of your foot-locker. They take another picture, and another joins the line. He leans over your shoulder to ask if you imagine real dress blues sit that way—tight at the throat—and you ask why your imagination would be any sharper than his. He stifles a laugh, then asks if you smiled for your picture. You ask through your teeth if he's serious. They shout for stillness and silence and more, and he breaks out in nervous laughter behind. They pull him out of line, and he laughs and laughs as they march him away. You fight the sudden urge to join him as another flash brightens the room.

Christopher Notarnicola's work has appeared in *AGNI*, *American Short Fiction*, *Bellevue Literary Review*, *Best American Essays*, *Chicago Quarterly Review*, *Image*, *River Teeth*, *The Southampton Review* and other publications. Find him in Fort Lauderdale, Florida and at christophernotarnicola.com.

OCCUR

JUDITH OSILÉ OHIKUARE

WHEN DID SHE EVEN OCCUR TO YOU?

Five years ago, at my old roommate's wedding while making Cincinnati chili. I performed a chiffonade on the corner of my thumb where nail met bed and dripped into the side salad before I could help it. She brought Band-Aids and damp paper towels so the cotton wouldn't stick. She squeezed to get the blood out; a sharpness rang in my hand and my head—which is where love and pain both occur.

WHEN DID YOU LAST SEE HER?

Monday night after burning cheap incense a man sold to me at a discount. He liked the tangles and whorls of my hair, he said, and threw in a jug of coconut oil that told me the temperature was above seventy-six degrees. I had wine too soon before sleeping. A smoky something wrapped me in gauze. Her mouth occurred to me: the thought, then the pressure. I spent Tuesday and last night trying to remember, ash gathering in the ceramic tray on my nightstand.

WHAT'S HER NAME?

I try not to tell people who don't already know. Gossip is wild and the world is small.

WHAT IS HER ISSUE?

The last time I assumed, she disappeared for months—hair changed, new number, apartment listed and let. I had to forget her, *hard*, so that she would come back. That kind of privacy had never occurred to me.

HOW DID YOU KNOW YOU WERE IN LOVE?

It felt as much like what I thought it should as it possibly could.

DO YOU MISS HER?

The thought had occurred.

Judith Osilé Ohikuare is a poet, writer, and Operations Director at NY Writers Coalition, a Brooklyn-based nonprofit that offers free creative writing workshops. She has performed at Lincoln Center's "Poets on the Plaza" and is a 2023 Fellow with In Surreal Life, the poet Shira Erlichman's "portable creativity school".

SELECTED GOOGLE SEARCHES REGARDING PETER JACKSON'S KING KONG

ABIGAIL OSWALD

IS KING KONG A HORROR MOVIE

It's true that the space between onscreen violence and your prone body can feel like safety. The horror is contained to a box, has an off switch. You are in the same room as the monster, yet also very far away.

If this is not your first viewing, then you already know how the story ends. Every forthcoming scream is a sound you've heard before.

But sometimes, even when we know exactly what's coming, we can still find ways to be afraid.

DOES KING KONG WIN

On the island, two monsters fight for dominance. The actress can't help but wonder what will be left of her when all of this is over.

WHY DOES KING KONG TAKE THE GIRL

The monster takes the actress; later on, the men take the monster. In a story like this, who is the true captive?

Stockholm syndrome was named for the hostages taken in a bank robbery in the eponymous city after they refused to testify against those who had detained them.

Later reports have suggested that this could be explained not by a particular sentiment of affection for said captors, but what appeared to be police disregard for the hostages' well-being in their response to the event in question. Both possibilities linked by fear of imminent death.

How often does survival come down to choosing the lesser of two evils?

Another truth: No matter which side you choose, you will still be hurt.

IS KING KONG A LOVE STORY

The actress nestles into the monster's hand after the longest day of her life. Survival has become uncertain, tied to likability. If she can make him laugh, he might let her live.

WHY DOES KING KONG DIE

You can map a hundred metaphors across a story like this; malleability is part of its appeal. But here is one truth: A monster in chains will always break free. Another: A monster who scales a city landmark must eventually descend.

Here, the fall occurs in slow motion. The actress sobs, overcome by an unexpected sense of loss.

A third truth: That which cannot be tamed must always be destroyed.

HOW DOES KING KONG END

A golden light streaks the horizon as darkness slips away. Beautiful, says the actress, and the monster follows her gaze. We, the audience, agree.

Abigail Oswald is a writer whose work predominantly examines themes of celebrity, crime, and girlhood. Her writing has appeared in *Catapult*, *Wigleaf*, *DIAGRAM*, *Split Lip Magazine*, and elsewhere. She holds an MFA from Sarah Lawrence College and currently resides in Connecticut. Find her online at abigail-washere.com.

AN EMPTY DAY

PAMELA PAINTER

A man has been walking past my home, past my
front window, every day now for two weeks, maybe
longer. He wears a raincoat that drags at his ankles
and carries a frayed tote bag. Always the same BBC
bag. I think it is the man who stood in line behind
me at the bank or perhaps it was the corner shop. It's
a small town, a village, a hamlet. I sound as if I've
been reading too many British mystery novels set in
small towns still capable of outsized mayhem. When
I moved here in the fall my daughter complained
that my house is too close to the street as are the
houses on either side of mine, twenty or so all in a
row like a child's set of building blocks. A short stone
walkway brings any visitor through my gate and to
my door with fifteen steps. I don't have visitors. My
daughter comes twice a year, which doesn't count.
The mailman says hello when I am in my front
garden pruning the roses. It is always late afternoon
when I see the man coming down the sidewalk. His
gait is slow, measured. His gaze attaches itself to
my front door until he is five steps away from my
gate, at which time he pointedly looks away. He

continues slowly on his walk, but I suspect he will be back. He seems to be planning something. It is almost too good to be true.

SORROW EVERYWHERE

PAMELA PAINTER

At first it was just light ash drifting down from somewhere. We didn't look up and we didn't ask. Children drew cartoons in the ash on the sidewalks, and my neighbor said it was good for cleaning windows—that and crumpled newspaper. For a week her windows glinted with the dazzle of clean glass. Then the ash wasn't light anymore and it seemed to be drifting sideways. My neighbor stood at our fence and called over that it was good for her roses, and probably for my hyacinths. The children measured out a hopscotch grid in the driveway and dusted off round stones. My husband lost interest in football and blamed it on poor TV reception.

Nothing seemed threatening. We went about our lives, to our offices and warehouses and schools. Newscasters swooped and glided in front of their digital weather maps, wearing brightly patterned dresses or silly ties. The government assured us that mail delivery would not be interrupted and that AI crews were assembled and at the ready. Banks ran out of bills larger than $20. We learned that small skirmishes in countries whose names we never knew came to a standstill and larger wars in countries we didn't remember slowly ground to a stop. You would think these global developments would bring some degree of pleasure, but that didn't assuage our grief. Grief is too strong a word for what we were feeling. My neighbor said this when she knocked on our door. She has always been helpful. We sat in the kitchen. Over coffee and later over wine, she said it probably wouldn't last—sorrow everywhere.

Pamela Painter is the award-winning author of five story collections. Her stories have appeared in *Fictive Dream*, *Flash Boulevard*, *Harper's Magazine*, *jmww*, *SmokeLong Quarterly*, and *The Threepenny Review*, and most recently in *Flash Fiction America*. Painter's stories received three Pushcart Prizes, were presented on National Public Radio, and staged by WORDTheatre.

ARTIFICIAL AUTONOMY

HELENA PANTSIS

When my daughter came to life I kissed her face. I told her to keep away from forks and toasters and electric sockets and bathtubs full of water unattended. I held her to her father, asked him to care, to kiss her cheeks and stroke her back as I did when she was born. He refused to look at her. He wanted a child of his own, with blood and skin and an appetite. My daughter couldn't understand, for though she didn't share his blood she could bear his name. She begged me to make things right, and I tried. I really tried. I cut my skin down the length of my womb so I could bear her, carried her in the core of my being to birth her like any other child would be born. But my husband was a man, and my daughter a machine.

He kept his names to himself, and my daughter remained uncalled. Still I kept her, hoping that her smarts, compounding by the day, and her interests programmed to replicate his and mine, would one day be enough. The neighbours scorned, and my husband refused to be seen with us. When she grew some more she graduated, she married, she had kids of her own, but my husband refused to see them. I learnt to call my daughter by a look on my face. Still she loved us, and though my husband never saw her she would ask after him when she'd call.

When we became old, and couldn't care for ourselves anymore, my daughter came home. She came to cook and clean and bathe our ageing bodies. My daughter, with not an inch of flesh to her name, making of us mortals something clean to look upon. My daughter held me, and the cool of her body warmed me, and I kissed her face for the both of us. But my husband refused to see her. And on the day he died we breathed a sigh. My daughter took me by the hand, pressed her circuitry to my chest. She said: You can be now, and I began to cry. The water touched my daughter's chest and sparks began to fly. I couldn't stop, and it was killing her, but still she held me. She held me and cooed. And I loved her, and she loved me too.

Helena Pantsis (she/they) is a writer and artist from Naarm, Australia. A full-time student of creative writing, they have a fond appreciation for the gritty, the dark, and the experimental. More can be found at hlnpnts.com.

THE FINAL GIRL PREPARES TO WATCH HER SEASON OF *AMERICAN HORROR STORY*

MEGHAN PHILLIPS

The actress hired to play her is too old. She was barely sixteen that weekend at Camp Broken Rock, and the actress, though young (Jesus, so young), is twenty-five. She is twenty-five years old and beautiful, of course, with long limbs and gigantic eyes. The actress reminds her of a deer. A deer's eyes flashing in headlights from the side of the road. A deer's broken body by the side of the road.

As a child, she loved Greek mythology. Prized her copy of *D'Aulaires'* over all other books. She favored stories of Artemis, the brave and wild huntress. Her favorite: a hunter stumbles upon Artemis bathing in a stream. She turns him into a deer, sets his own hounds upon him.

#

She had declined the offers from Ryan Murphy's people, declined the call she was pretty sure was from Ryan Murphy himself. The consulting credit. The associate producer credit. The money, enough to pay off both their student loans, the car loan. Enough for a vacation, the first since their frozen honeymoon in Rhode Island five years ago.

Her husband said he understood. No amount of money was worth, he stopped and waved his hand at her torso, as if everything she'd been through was locked there between her heart and her groin. He said he understood. He also said he was too tired after another night of drama club rehearsals to do anything more than eat a sandwich and go to bed. He said, Do we have to watch it tonight? He said, I can try to stay up if you want.

But he falls asleep before the theme music starts, and she is alone with herself. Her face reflected in the television screen, in the beautiful young actress pretending to be her.

#

When she was there in the woods, her friends already dead in the cabin the car the boat house the stream, she thought of Artemis. She thought of the story of Artemis and the deer as she ran, but she couldn't remember the whole story. Couldn't remember who was the deer or why. Still, she had pushed aside branches and tripped over roots and prayed, *oh Artemis, make me a deer.*

Meghan Phillips is the author of the chapbook *Abstinence Only* (Barrelhouse), and her stories have appeared in *HAD*, *Wigleaf*, *Split Lip Magazine*, and elsewhere. She was a 2020 National Endowment for the Arts literature fellow. Meghan lives in Manheim, PA, with her husband and kids.

RICE & SUGAR

CAMIL PIPERNI

My grandmother holds the chicken between her hands. It's late June, and she is sixteen. She brings it home, its rumpled feathers and small eyes. The softness of its skin. Her husband—my grandfather—tells her to cook it for dinner. She brings it to the kitchen, sets it against the sink. It looks up at her and cries, because no matter how old it is, it will always be a child. She looks down at it and cries, because there are scissors in her hands, and she does not want to hurt it. She will never want to.

She tells me this on a morning when the light hides behind clouds. She steps out as warmth begins to peek through the balcony. She tells me, *He suffered. I cried because we both did.*

The next day, I walk until the coconut trees appear on the empty lot. I take one in my hands and pull until it breaks and my hair is covered in dirt. It smells like the conditioner she keeps in the bathroom. I bring it back, heavy with water. I say, *I found this and didn't know what to do with it. If you ever want to use it or cook with it, I'm here.*

I don't speak about how it takes hours to wash off. I don't speak about the recipe I wanted to make: coconut milk, stirred in the kitchen that overlooks the ocean. I don't speak about the way the rice bubbles to the surface, each grain and piece of fruit soaking up the sweetness. How it reminds me of the sun, heating every inch of the living room, of the dried figs on the table by the entryway.

She tells me how she never likes my food because, she thinks, there are too many spices. I think about how she tells me she grew up: only her family's food, the vegetables her mother grew in the garden. I remember how I've never grown up with the food I cook now, that I see in the places I trace my blood back to. I remember how I barely want to eat anything else. I imagine the zucchini—*zucca*—she tells me her father gave to each family in the village. I remember how each time I cook, I remember love.

How each time I sit down at the table to eat her food, I remember it again.

Camil Piperni was raised in South Slope, Brooklyn. They write creative nonfiction and prose poetry, and were awarded three gold keys for memoir and poetry in the 2022 Scholastic Art & Writing awards. They are passionate about science education and are working to sow a garden this spring.

KINDLING

KEITH J. POWELL

I lived alone on an island in a Queen Anne Victorian that was always on fire. On the day I first moved in, the turret was already ablaze, puff, puff, puffing threads of dark smoke into the sky, like coded messages to a distant land. Some people might have balked at committing to such a unique fixer-upper, but they didn't see its generous view of the bay or the way its oriel windows caught the moonlight.

My days there always began the same. I'd trek down to the beach at dawn, returning with two pails full of ocean to douse the worst of the fire. Then I'd set to work with hammer and nail mending whatever had been devoured the day before. In the evening, I'd pat my clothes and hair for hidden embers and take my dinner down by the shore, soaking my tired feet in the lapping tide. Afterward, I'd doze in a rocking chair on the wraparound porch, savoring the crash of waves on the rocks and the salty bite of the sea breeze.

Little by little though, the Sisyphean rhythm of it all exhausted me. Soot began to cake painfully beneath my nails. Phantom heat from scorched gables singed off my eyelashes. Inhaled ash wizening my voice down to a choked rasp. And I was no carpenter, no mason. The fire took what it took and some days, the best I could do was slather green paint over the char and move on. Then, one morning I awoke to flames dancing at the foot of my bed, like an eager pup ready to play. And that was enough.

Sharing my home with an open fire was one thing, it was quite another to welcome those same flames into my bedroom.

With the resolve of the brokenhearted, I collected the few trinkets I hadn't yet sacrificed and carried them down to my rowboat. The fire had consumed my oars years before, so I kicked off against the rough sand and let the tide take me out to sea. Drifting toward a pale blue horizon, I looked back at the house that had been my home. The fire looked manageable from afar. Fires always do.

Keith J. Powell is a writer, editor, and co-founder of *Your Impossible Voice*. Find more at www.keithjpowell.com.

THE DREAM HE FORGOT

MARZIA RAHMAN

And the days smell like copper. And the nights like Star cigarettes and cheap sentiments. And the whistles come from the tea stalls, roadside cafés, a young man riding a motorcycle, a middle-aged drunk, cussing out the moon. A car window rolls down slowly, and a finger emerges, beckoning. A cheap hotel has no fragrance, no clean sheets, no white bathrobes, and only half-lit corridors leading to half-lit corners. A 10 by 12 feet room, and a torn picture of a nude girl on the wall. The bed creaks loudly for some time, and then silence, broken by— drip . . . drip . . . drip—floating from far away or nearby. A toilet flushes and a door slams shut. *Get up. Leave*—comes the command. Two hours. Five hundred-*taka*, one ripped note, taped with scotch tape in the middle. *Change it!* Fresh notes rustle in his hand as he takes the corridor that seems to go on and on like old classics. A copy of Dickens's *David Copperfield*, a home library, and his sister's Barbie doll with straight silky hair and long legs flash through his mind. He used to imagine himself as a doll. A doll with a red bindi, red lips, sari wrapped around his slim, slender figure. A woman in the mirror, happy and pretty. He can still hear the sound of shattering glass, the shouts, the cries, the whiplashes. And one morning, the shirts and trousers no longer fitted. Life on the streets is tough. Shameful. If lucky, one finds a friend or two, a new shelter where they all look alike, and dress alike. And in the mornings, he zigzags between the cars, begging, clapping, cursing. And during the nights, he dreams of a house with dolls and no glass. And in his dream, there is a wedding sometimes, family and friends showering rose petals on the bride and groom, going around a sacred fire, and chanting a prayer. With *achol* swaying in the late-night breeze and bangles tinkling, he walks down a narrow path, flanked by tin-roofed houses. A manhole behind. A lamppost ahead. He looks up and tries to remember what made him so happy last night!

Marzia Rahman is a Bangladeshi fiction writer and translator. Her writings have appeared in several print and online journals. Her novella-in-flash *If Dreams had wings and Houses were built on clouds* was longlisted in the Bath Novella-in-Flash Award in 2022. She is currently working on a novella.

BY THE SEA

FAYE RAPOPORT DESPRES

She couldn't deny who and what she was. Still, their admonitions echoed in her head until it hurt.

"You must be practical."

"Why not try law school?"

"How about a career in nursing?"

The pale sky hung above the rolling waves. A lone seagull floated in circles on the breeze, its backdrop blue with wisps of cloud.

She understood their concerns, of course. She'd probably be waiting tables or cleaning bathrooms for years. The life she wanted would be hard, full of rejection.

Yet even on the beach—without paint—she found herself drawing with a stick in the sand.

Faye Rapoport DesPres is the author of the memoir-in-essays *Message From a Blue Jay*, the *Stray Cat Stories* children's books, and the microfiction collection *Soul to Soul: Tiny Stories of Hope and Resilience* (forthcoming, Huntsville Independent Press 2023). She lives in Cambridge, Massachusetts with her husband Jean-Paul Des Pres.

ALIGHT

LEILA RENEE

Some rogue cigarette flew into my eye. It was my second time ever in New York City. The ember sizzled. It was July. I screamed. Mia rushed to find a bathroom. We fled South Street Seaport and zigzagged the city's shimmering expanse. My tears caught a glint of the bodies, the buildings. I mourned my sight. We were nineteen. We were alone. We had landed in the city after our father finally banished us from the house. He said we owed him an apology. We weren't sure for what. We ducked into a pizza place. White lights bathed empty booths. An aproned elder lounged alone behind the counter. His chest was a crime scene of mangled tomatoes. He saw our panic and didn't react, just sighed and pointed to the bathroom. Outside the night hung sparse and shadowed. The sweet of roasted cashews wafted west. Inside, the tiny bathroom glowed with grime. Tile and quiet cocooned us. Mia set her hand on my shoulder. Who the fuck, she seethed, throws burning things? I hovered the sink and rinsed my eye with the metallic tap. It stung with cold. We made our way out of the restaurant, giving the man profuse thanks. He did not acknowledge us. The light cloaked him. He looked damned and divine. The door dinged open, and the city swaddled us. We walked into the flickering night. Mia's hot palm petalled my eye as it gushed with involuntary tears. We were alone. We had spent the summer floating between places that were not ours. Smoldering things kept accosting us. And there were things we did not tell each other. The seaport heaved at our backs, and the East River ebbed with secrets. We left the man behind us, alight and alone.

Leila Renee earned her MFA in Creative Writing from Syracuse University. She received the 2021 Gulf Coast Prize in Fiction and the 2022 Shirley Jackson Prize. Leila has work in *McSweeney's*, *Prairie Schooner*, *Columbia Journal* and more. She is a Visiting Assistant Professor of English at Pacific Lutheran University.

LAUGH TRACK

MARIA ROBINSON

I read an article about the mind's eye. It's not something I'd ever thought much about, but apparently, if a researcher says, "Picture . . ." ("your breakfast table" or "the face of your lover"), most people can conjure an image vivid as a photograph. Not me. My mind's eye is like the beginning of *The Diving Bell and the Butterfly* or a short film by Brakhage—heavy on the flicker and blur, light on sharp edges. More like sunlit shadows filtered through an eyelid than something captured with a shutter-click.

I've been reading short stories by Lucia Berlin and having bad dreams all week. I don't think the two are related. But my little sister wrote an essay about my ex & me & my old dog Milo, and that might be. Just the other day it was ten years since Milo died. I texted a friend who knew us back then and said *Milo died ten years ago today* and he said *Wow! Time flies.*

Fug it, I replied. (*Tempus, that is.*)

Last night before bed something—a headline? a tweet? some fuckface on the news?—reminded me of that *Seinfeld* episode where a guy "took it out" in front of Elaine, how it was played for twenty-two minutes of guffaws, the whole laugh track hanging on the actors' intonations around "it" and "out." Then I fell asleep and had a dream my boyfriend got arrested for public masturbation. I woke up and kicked his foot away while my mind flickered and blurred with all the unsolicited dicks I've ever seen. Some were more unpleasant than others, but none were a delight. They all felt like yesterday. Suddenly a perfect sentence crackled through my twilit mind. It was gristly and crisp, and I knew by the way its arrival xylophoned up my spine that it was the predicate for some important future work, but I was too smothered in flickering dicks to write it down. I chanted it to myself instead, willing myself to remember in the morning. But when I woke, the only thing I could remember was *Seinfeld*. I tried to imagine it going another way. Elaine, wild-eyed, busts into the apartment and says, "He took it out." Jerry says, "It? . . . Out?" Elaine nods, eyes still wild. Jerry says, "Elaine, that's sexual assault!"

Picture it for me. Tell me where the laugh track would go.

Maria Robinson's work has appeared in *The Forge Literary Magazine*, *Catapult*, *New World Writing Quarterly*, *PANK*, *Bellevue Literary Review*, and *Cream City Review*, among others. Find her at mariarobinson.com.

SQUASH

MICHELLE ROSS

Every spring, I pollinate the squash. With a cotton swab, I transfer pollen from male flowers to female flowers. But when the first squash flowers bloom this March, pollination is a more painstaking effort. I save pollen from male flowers in a plastic sandwich bag in the tea towel drawer. The flowers' rhythm is all wrong. One morning, three female flowers atop stony green fruits open then close, their fruits withering with them. The next morning, a single male flower, its golden genes soon to be trapped inside its own withering.

The flowers' poor timing is funny at first, the way they keep missing each other, like characters in a rom-com. Like how alone in my car, stuck in traffic, I feel tender towards my husband. I run my fingers along the scar on my left arm, a line that marks a place where I was once open. Then I'm home, and there's dinner to prepare and clothes to fold. Also, the man I come home to isn't the man I imagined. He is less attentive, less considerate. He is less. This man puts his plate into the sink, the bright green buds of homegrown broccoli I roasted untouched. "Who put this broccoli into the sink?" I ask, assuming it was one of the kids. "It's just a few pieces. Who cares?" he says.

By late April, the flowers' poor timing unnerves me. Also, still no fruit, despite my efforts. I think of the verb form of *squash*—to flatten or crush.

One night, my husband pushes our pillows together, and his hands are too hot. They scald like the noon sun.

The next night, I lie there willing him to touch me, but his back is turned, he's snoring. I am a refrigerator, and he is a dull magnet that won't stick.

By late May, even the squash's limbs are limp, lifeless. Not once in all these weeks did a male flower and a female flower open simultaneously.

I say to my husband, "It's as if they were willfully trying to deny me fruit."

My husband says nothing. He pokes at his phone.

I say, "What if this is the end? What if there's no more fruit ever again?"

By the time my husband looks up from his phone, I've gone outside. Through the glass door, I watch his mouth open then close as I uproot the dead.

WHAT I OWNED

MICHELLE ROSS

In the little rust-red house, there were six rooms if you counted everything but the closets and the tiny laundry area sandwiched between the kitchen and the backyard. The only room I ever thought I owned, though, was the wood-paneled bedroom across the hall from the bathroom. Then my brother was born, and my little sister moved in with me. Then no room in that house was mine.

I spent most of my time outside where no one owned anything.

I don't mean the backyard. That belonged to Dad. He built the chicken coop. He built the pig pen, the turkey pen, the shed. He hoed the land to plant the vegetable garden. He dug the big hole that became the catfish pond. He built the bridge that went to the island in the middle of that pond. He built the deck from which we jumped into that muddy water to swim with those catfish, also Dad's, and whose whiskers tickled our toes.

I don't mean the garage. That was where Dad kept his tools and his leftover wood scraps. The garage was where he hung deer from a hook in the ceiling and stripped them of their fur and guts.

I don't mean the front yard, either. Dad owned the rock garden with the aloe that we rubbed onto scorched skin. He owned the oak trees, the chinaberry trees, the juniper trees. Those were his stakes in the ground that held up the smallest of those trees, uprighting it after a hurricane tried to knock it down. Dad owned the dirt and the grass. He owned the ditches that filled with water and crawdads every time it rained.

Truth was that Dad owned every room in the house, too. No room had ever really been mine.

No room in that house had ever really been my mother's, either, not that I concerned myself then with what my mother did or didn't own.

I spent most of my time in the woods behind our house. No one owned the blackberry bushes that scraped my legs. No one owned the banana spiders that spun hardy webs stretching from tree to tree. No one owned the ticks or the chiggers or the snakes. No one owned the lightning bugs that blinked on and off at dusk. Although flags toothpicked it, I didn't believe yet that anyone could really own the moon.

Michelle Ross is the author of the story collections *There's So Much They Haven't Told You* (2017), *Shapeshifting* (2021), and *They Kept Running* (2022). Her work is included in *Best Small Fictions*, *Flash Fiction America*, and other anthologies. She is fiction editor of *Atticus Review*.

LUCK/HISTORY

C.C. RUSSELL

The truth of it is how lucky, how astonishingly fortunate we were. That car in the rain coming out of nowhere, the drinking glasses thrown against walls in our most awful moments. Everything that we ingested, everything that we refused. Every part of us that we shattered. Rolling on those icy roads, walking the highway that night as we tripped—how beautiful the oncoming headlights always were. That bridge above the train tracks and how it would shake while we casually talked about jumping. How beautiful everything was that could end us. But it didn't. Call it mercy or luck. Call it what you will, but I can look at the light on the side of your face. I can call. We are still here.

C.C. Russell writes from just below the mountains in Wyoming where he lives with a collection of humans and rescue cats. Links to more of his work can be found at ccrussell.net.

HARDY HOLDS COURT AT THE CORNER STORE

KRISTINA T. SACCONE

His old man puts him on the afternoon shift. *Says it keeps me outta trouble.* Hardy's behind the counter, sells a six-pack to someone's uncle and a can of motor oil to the guy who teaches shop. When we show up, he takes payment in autumn leaves. The system goes: a golden leaf gets you a nickel. Red or orange is just a penny. Multicolored ones—he calls them *Platinums, baby*—gets you the nickel plus a single Camel Light.

All of us go wild when the trees start to turn. Someone's mama shouts from her Buick: *Why you boys monkeying in the trees?* We're just hunting for platinums. It's easier than getting a weekend job or sliding a few bucks from Pops' wallet. But they have to be real gems. No nicks. No blemishes. *Yeah kid, the caterpillar eggs look cool but it don't get you a nickel*, he says to me. Bring anything brown and he won't let you in the store for a week.

Hardy's little sister sits next to me in biology class, says he ships them to a sweetheart in California, where they don't get colors on their trees. But one night, just before dinnertime, I find a real sharp platinum. He's behind the store over a rusty bucket, flames popping. He trades me for a nickel and a smoke, tosses me the lighter, feeds the platinum to the fire and says: *Sometimes I like to see beautiful things burn.*

Kristina T. Saccone (she/her) writes short fiction and nonfiction. She is an MFA candidate at Randolph College, and she edits *One Wild Ride*, a limited-run online literary journal about caring for our aging parents. She lives in the Washington, DC area with her son, partner, and two small dogs.

BANANA BOAT

AURELEO SANS

Mz. Chiquita, her rattle-bones are slick with oil pressed from coconut, her bananas are sharpened and firm. A steelpan choir booms. She counterfeits dance. The fruit in her basket hat are fake, hollow. White flesh and breasts and ass already melted in the sun. The banana queen stirs a flame. The fire licks at hope. She's paid to distract the men from their toil. Her toil is their toil. She is a piece of company machinery like the steamship, a deathship always waiting for its cargo, salivating sea foam. The men are eager to return home, but the urgent, unripened piles wait to be sorted and dispatched. The bananas are an unyielding march of stretched tears down a human conveyer belt. Platters of the fruit weigh down workers' head, others wrap around, constrict shoulders. The neck is for lifting. The body, for sacrifice. All men in line, all waiting to unload their loads, all wanting to return home. They know only fair-skinned Atlases can shrug.

Mz. Chiquita sounds a tin bugle no one hears because the men have started to sing. Her job is vital. She knows that the wealthy blancos need sweetness, to them all the sweeter knowing it comes at the expense of life. The line leads to the dock leads to the vessels. Slave ships and galleons have never left but these fruit will. They are going for a cruise. They are meant for a new world. This Old World is salt, not sweet. It murders the men's wives, the men's children. It is tradition.

But this time is different. This air is different because of the submachine guns and the ammo. Because Mz. Chiquita is slipping on peels. She is trying to beat a war drum but she's mislaid rhythm. She is losing the beat. She is playing xylophone on her bones but the music has abandoned her. Her phalanges fall to the floor.

Dark becomes light. The sun is peeking now, pinkening, ready to roast. Daylight's come and the workers are ready to return home. The ships are ready to sink. The workers ready to strike.

STAMPS

AURELEO SANS

We've gotta arrive at the DSS office an hour early
on the day they give out food stamps or else we will
be there all day, and nobody is happy, and everybody
is whining including Mamá, who's saying *why did
I cross the Caribbean to come to this mentiroso country*
as she stuffs the girls into jackets like reluctant
dolls; they've got to come along because you don't
leave babies by themselves, even though we all wish
for bed when the light on the bus that early in the
morning is too much yellow, and our eyes have too
much crust, and on my index finger, I look at the
yellow crust in the yellow light, and I dream of a gold
rush and how having money can change everything
but we have no money and that's why we ride on a
bus that stinks and why we stand in single file and
why I swallow every last bit of gold; meanwhile, our
position in the snaky line goes from the rattle to the
stomach to the fangs: the non-smiling lady behind
the glass barrier, who hides her eyes and slips us
the stamps; in my mind, I've already teleported to
our next bus stop: Swanson's, where we sort through
about-to-expire perishables and irregular items for

treasures at discounted prices; once we found bacon-wrapped filet mignon; once we found shampoo that smelled like bear bottle honey but right now we are sizing up dimpled cans of fruit cocktail and Vienna sausages, Mamá says, *life is about balance; it's like these cans; you've got to pick the cheapest ones with the fewest number of dents*, and I tell her that Mrs. Grimmer, the social studies teacher, said messed up cans can kill people, but she says *no te preocupes* and she's right; the cans are not what's going to kill us anyways and not that we care because after Swanson's, we play Monopoly with the leftover stamps instead of the cash the game is missing.

---

aureleo sans is a Colombian-American, queer, formerly unhoused writer with a disability, living in San Antonio, Texas. In 2022, she was a Sewanee Writers' Conference Scholar, a Tin House Scholar, a Lambda Literary fellow, and a Periplus fellow. Her work has appeared in *Shenandoah*, *Electric Literature*, *Passages North*, and elsewhere.

YOUR CHILDHOOD BEST FRIEND GETS HER HANDS ON SOME QUESTIONABLE DOPE

JASMINE SAWERS

That's it. That's the story.

Or:

She was six years old with hair the color of a summer sunset over Lake Erie the first time you saw her. She grabbed your hand and pulled you into a new world called Emriolan. She was not a princess but a knight; you were not a dragon to be slain but a dragon to be flown, to be pointed in the direction of enemy armies, to be the protector of the kingdom of her freckled body.

The two of you roved the countryside rescuing damsels and razing tyrants for many years, until she grew too old for Emriolan. Too old for adventures. Too old for a terminally uncool baby like you.

You are twenty-nine when you receive an invitation to her Facebook memorial page. You imagine her crossing the border into Emriolan, where she can blaze, magnificent, forever. You spend a week scribbling in a notebook all the things you and she did there. When that's full, you pull another from the shelf and begin to write.

Sir Emily of Clan Dervishon was hiding a dragon egg.

You save her, over and over again.

Jasmine Sawers is a Kundiman fellow and Indiana University MFA alum. Their work has appeared in many fine journals and won awards from *Ploughshares*, *NANO Fiction*, and *Fractured Lit*. Their book, *The Anchored World*, was a finalist for the 2023 PEN/Robert W. Bingham Prize for Debut Short Story Collection.

54.7754° N, 31.7890° E, APRIL OF 1940

SLAWKA G. SCARSO

Tucked in the pockets of their wool coats, medals pinned to their breasts and officer stripes to their shoulders, the prisoners clutch us, grasp us, feeling our comforting shape in the palm of their hands and through their fingers, the way they would do with the folds of their prayer books, and the photos of their wives, their children, their parents, their lovers.

Tucked in their pockets, they feel our curves and our dents, as the train gains speed, ta-taaa, ta-taaa, ta-ta-ta-ta-taaa, leaving Kozelsk behind. *We're going home*, they all think without saying it out loud, because that would bring bad luck. *We're going home*, they all think, until one of them, bored of looking at the foggy forests outside the window, notices a carving in the wood panel. One made with one of us, with one of our dents. "*Pociąg jedzie na północ, a nie na zachód*. The train is going North, not West," it says. West being home, North God knows where.

As the voice spreads, and the fog dissipates, the sun disclosing the truth of the orientation, however debated the destination and the date will be for decades, they clutch us like rosary beads, and pray.

But we're not rosaries, we're just the keys to their houses that they kept because they hoped to be home soon, and are now empty, because their families were asking too many questions: *where are our husbands, our fathers, our brothers?*

Soon we will lose our smooth curves, our dents rusting in the damp soil, trees carefully planted on top of us, to conceal those who are concealing us, tucked with their fading hopes in the pockets of their wool coats.

STAY AS LONG AS YOU NEED

SLAWKA G. SCARSO

From outside, it looks like any ordinary shop, with the products neatly organized. The prams are in one corner, because they are bulkier, and the cots, too; there are tiny baby blankets you can't resist touching, and blue-and-green pajamas printed with dinosaurs and stars, and rubbery toys, and bibs and nappies, and all the things that you most likely have already bought for a friend's baby, whether you were trying to be sensible at the time and picked something useful or wanted to be the fun auntie, even though your friend wasn't your sister, but—you know— she thought you'd appreciate being called like that.

When you go inside, nobody will try to approach you to sell you something right away. Shop assistants will say *Good morning* and smile like they mean it, because they do, and they're all well-mannered there. And because they took that extra class of customer care that everyone else skips in the other baby shops.

Nobody will ask you how far into pregnancy you are, or when the baby is due. They won't eye your belly, and they won't judge, but they will look you in the eye, and they will say that you can stay as long as you need. They will offer you tea and a cookie. You will walk around the aisles, touch the fluffy blankets, hold the cuddly toys, take the empty pram for a gentle spin. And when you are done, you will stop at the cashier and leave a little something, depending on how long you needed to stay. Because nothing is on sale at the Pretend Baby Shop. Because some things cannot be bought.

Slawka G. Scarso's work has appeared in *Ellipsis Zine*, *Ghost Parachute*, *Fractured Lit*, *Scrawl Place* and elsewhere. Her novella-in-flash *All Their Favourite Stories* was commended in the 2022 Bath Novella-in-Flash Award and published by Ad Hoc Fiction. She is based in Italy. More words on www.nanopausa.com.

WARMUP

E.J. SCHWARTZ

Half the Jews at Congregation Beth El get their noses broken by Dr. Mendelson under general anesthesia. You can tell by our matching nostril scars. They're faint and patted with green concealer to cover any redness rising to the surface of our skin.

I was fifteen when I took a hammer to the face. Emma Goldbaum went first and we spent the early months with our super straight noses in sunscreen-white casts. Now, in the back of our Hebrew school classroom—one clock ticking to U.S. time, the other ticking to Israel's—we paint our nails Geranium red. A square fat TV flashes piles of emaciated bodies onto our T-shirts, and we ignore the footage from Auschwitz as we blow air through our circled lips, waiting for the color to harden.

"I'd give anything to be that skinny," Emma whispers as she stares at the dead bodies. I keep my fingers flat-to-dry on the brown laminate desk and occasionally peer up at the barbed wire fences onscreen.

Hannah C leans over to us, picking a scab textured like rock candy. "Did it hurt?" She lets her hair drape across her left eye like a blackout curtain, like she doesn't want us to see how Jewish she is from the side. "Your noses?"

"Not one bit," Emma lies.

"Only a little," I admit.

The Holocaust video is paused by our saggy-eyed Rabbi and we mark our seats with our jackets to take a water break. I scrape my fresh nail polish into goo and flick it down the water fountain drain. The nail beds are dyed orange, but I'll just reapply a fresh coat over top for the second half of the show.

In act two, babies are plucked like thorns from their parents' arms and a woman weeps close to the camera so I can see the pores on her hooked nose. The smell of acetone leaves me dizzy enough not to feel anything and *we're not like her anyway*, says my super-straight nose. My hands lift toward the blueish TV light as if the screen is a fire and I can feel the warmth on my hands from the dead bodies only a few feet away. Like this is just a warmup for whatever comes next, and when they come for us again, they won't find anything we haven't already erased.

E.J. Schwartz's writing has appeared in *The New York Times*, *Barrelhouse*, *Necessary Fiction*, and elsewhere. Her debut novel, *Before We Were Blue*, won the 2022 IPPY gold medal in Young Adult Fiction, and was a Foreword INDIES Book of the Year Awards finalist. She tweets @byejschwartz.

LONG AFTER THE LONG RIDE INTO THE SUNSET

MARVIN SHACKELFORD

First thing in the morning I draw a blue mark in the shallow dimple of my cheek, so near my mouth I sometimes taste it. The air is curious just before sunrise, darker and cooler, and I dress a little too warm, too safe. My hands shake, pulling wool from the hanger. The house sleeps. Outside, the birds begin to speak. They're excited, warning of something. I lie on the porch and hold my hand out away from the sun. I study its shadows disappearing. I flex my fingers and clutch them tight, find the tendons and sinew where they hide. When I make a fist they smooth away again, but my arm begins to ache. Ponies out on the plain throw their heads and stumble to their next day. I listen to their strange decisions, hoof and nicker, always in flight. They grow from gray-and-white ages past, carefree dreams, to finely pointed patches of color, clear outlines quickly separating the world. They disappear, pieces and the whole. The house still sleeps but I rise into it. I line a skillet with thickly sliced bacon, applewood, and the rooms fill with smoke. It's the idea of breakfast, and it's only a matter of time. I check the many bodies in their beds, see them start to swell and turn, and revisit the mirror. I'm still beautiful, the mark still there, and all our life sits neatly, nearly as we placed it. Almost unchanged, but not quite.

Marvin Shackelford is the author of *Field Guide to Lonely Birds* (stories, Red Bird Chapbooks) and *Endless Building* (poems). His work has appeared in *The Kenyon Review*, *New Ohio Review*, *trampset* and elsewhere. He resides in Southern Middle Tennessee, working as a caretaker of persons, places, and things.

MY UNCLE LIVED IN THE FUTURE

PARTH SHAH

He mailed the paperwork when I was still an orca. The hungry days. Unyielding seasons of screaming water. Mother obsessed over deciphering their sound, preoccupied when kinfolk sank to the rocks. I died in the alien net before we could learn the language, and I became his nephew. My rebirth is at a hospital close to the ocean and close to the post office where he mailed off the forms. My uncle comes in the morning to hold me, dressed in his customary polo and slacks, square glasses with silver frames like beams of a bridge. He built bridges for the state, one in every county. Always building, unable to ignore connections. My uncle lived in the future. Itineraries were his prose. He planned sweet sixteens, sangeets, he edited college essays and filed taxes. He engineered the visa process for relatives and friends and strangers, including my parents. My parents. He didn't ask if they wanted to come. He learned their names and saw a fate outside of una. They didn't know english but they could speak two languages already, a third would be an easy extension, especially with a television. I saw him the other day on the train, an orb of buttery light hovering by my seat as we crossed the seabridge over my grave. My uncle lay in bed that last year, watching movies, immobilized by his tired lungs. I gave him the password to my netflix. For his profile, he chose an avatar that looks like a bollywood policeman, aviator sunglasses and a handlebar mustache. He was always clean shaven. When black hairs started to accompany my whiteheads, and some aunty caught me kissing a swim teammate at a matinee, my uncle told me on this land I can choose who I want to be, but once I choose, I must memorize my script.

Parth Shah earned his MFA in fiction from the University of Wyoming. His audio stories have been broadcast on NPR programs including *All Things Considered*, *Morning Edition*, *Throughline*, and *Hidden Brain*. He is a teacher, a home cook, and an indoor-outdoor cat.

WHAT THE MIRROR TELLS YOU

GAIL LOUISE SIEGEL

You lie in bed under the quilt from your son and his wife, and stare at the ceiling. It's impossible to sleep while your roommate groans. You think the same thoughts every night. That it's hard to believe what the mirror tells you. The wrinkles and spots. The thin, limp, gray hair. You can't reach your feet—or if you can, your hands shake too badly to clip a hangnail. That woman frowning back at you is a stranger, an alien.

Trapped in this awful body, they park you at a table with a seat-mate who seems to dust his pasta with dandruff instead of parmesan. After every meal, dessert is the same watery bowl of tepid aged plums, and Greta Johnson from Room 207 in the Memory Wing plays the same nocturne in the lounge over and over again until you want to flip the heavy black keyboard cover onto her hands and crush them.

It will do no good, not even if you break her fingers, because you are haunted by her scales and trills in the bath and in your dreams. So you nod at her and smile weakly at her balding cap of white frizz. You picture Greta Johnson on an amphitheater stage, an old lady glowing under a spotlight, wearing a tuxedo and fuzzy pink slippers. But what kind of person is in there, really? A concert pianist, a jazz club crooner, a retired music teacher?

Every day you mean to ask her, and every day you forget.

Gail Louise Siegel's short-shorts have appeared in journals including *Brevity, Post Road, Salamander, StoryQuarterly, Wigleaf, New World Writing Quarterly,* and *Elm Leaves Journal.* Longer work can be found in places such as *Ascent, The North Dakota Quarterly, Zoetrope All-Story Extra* and *FRiGG.* She has an MFA from Bennington College and lives just outside of Chicago.

BONE ON BONE

ERIC SCOT TRYON

My son starts grinding his teeth in the fall of third grade. As he sleeps. The scraping, the pressure—I hear it through the thin walls of our shoebox in the Tenderloin. Our third apartment this year. He in the bedroom, me on the couch. It keeps me up all night. Just as I'm finally adapting to our walls made pink by the neon flicker of Peaches, the strip club across the street.

I ask him one morning, *Are you okay? Does anything hurt?* Head down, shoveling stale Cheerios, he shakes his head.

The grinding intensifies each night. That crunch, heavy like cement. In the fitful space between waking and sleeping, I dream his teeth fly out of his mouth and shoot across the room one by one. Not fragments, but whole teeth. Adult teeth, with long red sinewy roots that trail behind like streamers. I wake with a screaming headache.

Again I ask in the morning, *Are you okay?* Lifting his head from his cereal, he looks at me, nods, and wipes a bit of old milk from his chin.

I buy him a mouthguard from CVS. He refuses to wear it. The grinding continues. Like the shifting of tectonic plates, a pressure that could move continents. Amplified by a father's guilt, when it reaches my ears it jackhammers. And with Peaches still winking her neon nipples at me through the paper thin drapes, I can't sleep for days.

I return to CVS. Buy ear plugs, a night mask, Jack Daniels. At night, I bury my head in the thrift store couch cushions, breathing in decades of cigarettes and other people's sweat.

I have to see it for myself. To watch him sleep, my son, my small boy, making these horrific sounds that shake our fragile walls. Just past midnight, I stand in his doorway and wait for my eyes to adjust. *Bone on bone.* The grinding now accented by squeaks and clicks. My eyes adapt, and there he is. Asleep. Eyes clenched like fists. His teeth and the bones in his face grinding and shifting, popping and dislocating, rearranging themselves. Desperately trying to reconfigure into a different little boy, one who lives in an apartment where the walls are still white, one whose father makes fruit salad in the morning: fresh apples and mangoes and peaches.

I'M A HONDA ODYSSEY, I'M A CHRYSLER VOYAGER

ERIC SCOT TRYON

I pick up Jeremy from school at 2:50. I receive a chrome straight-razor shaving kit for Father's Day. I have sex on birthdays, anniversaries, and that one time she went to Margarita Monday with her friends. I paste popsicle sticks together with Marissa to look like a California mission. I use words like refinance, cold front, and energy efficient. If I arrive at Jeremy's school even a minute after 2:35, I'm in the back of the pick-up caravan and will sit for an hour. I will be irritated the rest of the evening. I spend three days putting up Christmas lights. I put my mom in an assisted-living facility that neither she nor I can afford. I feel bloated after my third beer. The California mission looks nothing like Marissa had envisioned, and she spends the rest of the night in tears. On Facebook, I see my high school girlfriend is going through her second divorce. I have more black socks than white. I receive wood-handled bar-b-que tools branded with my initials for Father's Day. I lose to Jeremy for the first time playing one-on-one on the driveway hoop. When co-workers ask me how my three-day weekend was I say, "Not long enough" and replay the exchange in my head the rest of day. I look forward to masturbating in the shower. I check the weather daily. I sing Disney songs with Marissa and know more words than her. I take my family to Yosemite in July. My back hurts for three days after Jeremy beats me at hoops. I have almost paid off my student loans. But not quite. I start snoring. I ignore that occasional pain in my chest. I still love my wife. I'm a vasectomy. I'm a Roth IRA. I'm a golf towel.

Eric Scot Tryon is a writer from San Francisco. His work has appeared or is forthcoming in *Glimmer Train*, *Ninth Letter*, *Willow Springs*, *Los Angeles Review*, *Sonora Review* and elsewhere. Eric is also the Founding Editor of *Flash Frog*. Find more information at www.ericscottryon.com.

A QUEER GIRL'S GUIDE TO READING FAIRY TALES

REBECCA TURKEWITZ

You may root for the maiden to go deeper into the woods. You may root for the witch. You may hope that the glass slipper will fit, or not fit. You may ask the story three questions, so long as you do not expect a response. You may envy the damsel her tower, which keeps out the world, and the men that circle like wolves, and the townspeople who keep saying how pretty her hair is, how fair. You may hate the damsel's tower, and you may hate the damsel, and you may love her, and you may see that she and you are kin.

You may run your hands over the illustrations of the moon and the gnarled branches and the fiddle-playing cat. You may smell the forest-floor scent of the book's pages. You may crack the book's spine.

You may imagine yourself as Cinderella every time you sweep the kitchen or scrub the stubborn grease from a pan or scrape ice from your girlfriend's car. You may imagine yourself as Red Riding Hood while you cut through the overgrown park on your way home from work, or the bar, or a bad Tinder date. You may imagine yourself as the prince, or the sea witch, or the imp who will not give his name, or the wicked stepsister, or the woodsman, or the fool.

You may imagine yourself to be any of these characters, with their beauty or their bravery or their slyness or their treachery or their loneliness or their sweet giant axe. But if you keep reading, and if you read deeper and softer and in the arms of a foggy night, and if you let the outlines of the stories go blurry—just as you once let the outlines of the world go blurry so you could find your way into yourself— you will see that, actually, you are the spindle. You are the pricked finger and the drop of blood. You're the howling wind in the valley, and you are the cave. You are not the fox, but you are its greed. You're the red cloak in the shape of a girl, and you're the blade of the axe. You are every part of the forest that is not on the path. You're the spinning wheel. You're the promise. You're the gold.

Rebecca Turkewitz's debut collection of stories, *Here in the Night*, is forthcoming from Black Lawrence Press in July 2023. Her fiction and humor have appeared in *The Normal School*, *The Masters Review*, *SmokeLong Quarterly*, *The Cincinnati Review*, *The New Yorker's Daily Shouts*, and elsewhere. She lives in Portland, Maine.

AN EIGHT FOOT POSSUM

EVAN WILLIAMS

An eight foot possum by the lake played dead, but only seven feet of it. The other foot dragged the body behind it, dragged it nearer the lake. The waves weren't there, had disappeared overnight. It all looked like a waterpark tide pool the manager hadn't started up for the day. The one foot of possum stopped dragging his other seven feet toward the water and slumped. "I'm exhausted," he said to the no-wave lake. I sat with him. The possum looked at me like an alive possum looks. "I'm cold," the final foot of beating-heart-possum said. I helped him wind seven feet of dead possum around his shoulders like a blanket. We sat until the waves on the lake came home.

THE CIRCLE IS A PART OF THE HOLE

EVAN WILLIAMS

On his day off, the telemarketer receives a call from a telemarketer. What are you selling, the telemarketer asks the telemarketer who's called. I'm not, the telemarketer calling responds, I'm assembling a team. Only the best and the brightest and the nimblest dialing fingers. We're going to call every phone number in the world in record time. I've got a garage full of phone books just in case we get lost, but I figure we can start at 000-000-0001. The telemarketer who'd been called on his day off checked the number calling. 000-000-0000. Who are you, the telemarketer asks the telemarketer who's called him on his day off. The phoning telemarketer says only, I am the sound a telephone makes before it learns to ring.

Evan Williams is a queer writer living in Chicago. They are a co-founder of the temporary journal *Obliterat* and author of the chapbook *Claustrophobia, Surprise!* (HAD Chaps). More of Evan's work can be read in *DIAGRAM*, *Pleiades*, *Bennington Review*, and elsewhere.

OWEN WILL TELL YOU

FRANCINE WITTE

that his name begins with a zero and not the letter O. He will insist that you need to know this. It explains me, he will say.

People are always correcting him. Go ask your mother, they will laugh. He will breathe deep and tell them he is motherless. Found on a doorstep, like he was. I began with a zero, and the name just followed. This is where most people walk away.

Right now, Owen with a zero is at a job interview. The thirtieth this month. Everything will go fine until Owen brings up the story of his name.

But this time is different. The interviewer's name is Sally, whose name is spelled with a dollar sign and not the letter S. Her mother was a prostitute, her father a ten-dollar trick. She says that people assume she's a gold-digger, and how it has nearly ruined her life.

When Owen hears this, he goes instantly squishy with love. Sally hires him on the spot, both for the job and as her husband.

Years from now, their children will have no name

issues. And if Owen has anything to say about it, they won't even have any names.

Francine Witte's recent books are *Dressed All Wrong for This* and *Just Outside the Tunnel of Love* (Blue Light Press), *The Way of the Wind* (Ad Hoc Fiction), and *The Cake, The Smoke, The Moon* (ELJ Editions). She is flash fiction editor for *Flash Boulevard* and *The South Florida Poetry Journal.*

SHINE IN HER LIGHT

SABINA Y. WONG

Come with me, and I'll take you places, she whispered after another magical evening. The announcement would come out in the paper a week after the man hitched a line to the end of her tail and they were long gone from the night sky: *Man Marries Comet*. Hurtling through space was exhilarating. One moment Earth was beside them, and before he knew it, they were in distant reaches he'd only seen in pictures. Each year they approached his former planet, and his heart swelled with pride imagining all the discussion surrounding them as the trail-blazers making history with their union.

On their tenth anniversary, however, he found he could no longer muster the same level of excitement. *Why were they always so eager to see* her? he thought, watching the crowds gather to see the meteor shower left in her wake. *There are other comets, but there are no other men married to one.* I'm *the first.* When they returned, he needed to take matters into his own hands to share the glory once again.

His wife's trajectory wobbled, and she turned with

alarm to watch her husband inch his way along the cord. *Stop!* she cried. But he kept climbing. She probably warned him off because she wanted all the acclaim for herself. He smiled when they dipped closer to Earth because it would provide the best opportunity for people to see him in detail, so he scrambled closer to his wife who kept urging him to return to his original position.

Together, they skimmed Earth's atmosphere. Combined with their speed, the heat created stung his knee. He yelped, and tried to shimmy back down, but by then it was too late—the high temperature fused his skin to the rope. His cries were drowned out by the *oohs* and *aahs* of the people watching the comet transform into a shooting star—the first to have done so—resulting in scientists writing about the event for years to come. In a blaze of white hot fire, they crashed into the Earth, where enthusiasts caravanned out to comb the area. They found her, just a tiny thing in the desert, reduced down to a tenth of her size, but no less grand. They wrapped her in linens to transport her to a museum, where throngs of people would flock to see her, while the man's ashes scattered in the sand.

Sabina Y. Wong (she/her) lives in a tiny apartment in Los

Angeles made from the hundreds of books in her TBR. Her works are featured in *Full House Literary*, *Provenance Journal*, *GASTROPODA*, *Janus Literary*, and *The Citron Review*. Another piece is forthcoming in Gutslut Press.

LAST TIME

DOUGLAS A. WRIGHT

For the last time, my brother and I are together. We are sitting in the dark with the blue flicker of the TV screen, playing Super Nintendo in the basement of our parents' house where he lived like a child, a patient, a secret. The hole in the drywall has been patched, the paint weeks dry, white, the faint ghost of its imprint still there, a slapdash attempt at erasing the night when my mother heard the thunder down the stairs, the wrecking-ball crash, his head split open with all that blood and her arms cradling him like a child, a patient, a secret.

We are pretending everything is normal. We are experts at this, patching disaster and painting it white. We are taking turns dying, trading the controller back and forth. He must've beaten Super Mario World a hundred times—sober, stoned, interstellar on dextromethorphan (his drug of choice, post oxy)—but we are playing it from the beginning so we can beat it together, with dispatches of words hanging in the air like dust in a fallout shelter.

"I'm alright," he says.

He's not alright.

"Last time," he says.

He's dying over and over on the same level, a haunted castle, slipping into the lava, respawning at the gate outside, caught in a loop, with no memory of what happened before. And then, like lightning, he's in the flow, his eyes disked, blue sky eclipsed by the widening darkness of his pupils—fearless, leaping across pits, dodging fireballs and spiked pillars, eating mushrooms and feathers, feeling invincible in a frantic mad dash to the end. And then he dies and dies again, and I die and die again, mashing buttons in that final moment of panic.

I don't want to leave my brother, but my friend is having a party and I want to go. He says it's okay. So we hug for a long time because we always hugged like that whenever I left him, because I never knew if it would truly be the last.

Douglas A. Wright is a fiction writer and screenwriter living in Brooklyn with a mischievous rabbit named Hazel and too many books. His stories have appeared in *Vestal Review*, *Stanchion*, *Fictive Dream*, *Jabberwock Review*, *Oyster River Pages*, and *OffBeat Magazine* among others. He is the founding editor of *EXCERPT Magazine*.

MY MOTHER VISITS ME IN AMERICA AND IS OFFENDED BY WHAT THE DISHWASHER CAN DO

TARA ISABEL ZAMBRANO

She asks if there's a human inside, who scrubs the dishes and puts them back as they came in. I laugh, kiss her on her forehead, dipping my nose into her thinning hair.

I smear creamy lotion on my mother's calloused palms, white settles in the trench of her lifeline. Years of washing dishes for restaurants, to send me to school, to buy books and uniforms after Pa died. Her back curved over dhobi ghats, wringing out towels and sheets. Her long face against the fabric on the clothesline, siphoning damp relief. Now, next to the sink where she has rinsed her life, a dishwasher is draining erasure into the creases on her forehead. During the day, she sticks her finger in the turrets of silverware holders, presses the soap pellets on her wash-annulled palms, their scent embroidered into her shadow. After dinner, her rosary-shaped eyes wait until the red LED of the machine turns off, expecting someone to walk out drenched in water, laced in froth.

"I haven't embraced the porcelain in days," she complains, her eyes dull with boredom. "My limbs are sore from underuse."

"Ma, I have it all so you can rest now!" I plunge my gloved hands into the greasy dishwater in the sink, a mechanical whirring of the motor starting in the background.

"I wake up at night," my mother says, "and grow sad about the world. It's dying because there's too much smartness and not enough touch."

I shake my head and hear the mushy hurt of her guts—deep breaths, snotted air, a washcloth-cringed wetness split between us.

"It's a curse not to use your gift to serve. Besides what do you do your entire life if not clean? First, the skin for good health, then the tongue with silence, and last, the mind with compassion," my mother says.

I don't know what to say, so I interlace my fingers in hers. They don't fit as they once did. There are gaps from which the light escapes.

Tara Isabel Zambrano is a writer of color and is the author of a full-length flash collection *Death, Desire, And Other Destinations*, published by Okay Donkey Press in 2020.

UNSTABLE RELATIONSHIP

LUCY ZHANG

We're making papier-mâché birds in art class, ripping strips of newspaper and smearing glue over our fingers. Albatross females lay only one egg, and those whose eggs don't hatch end up in bird divorce. The more efficient of us have time to make eggs, although it's too hard to maintain the round shape with crinkled paper, and they end up lopsided and lumpy, like tier-three fruits rejected by Whole Foods and sold at $0.29/lb. at the local farmers' market, but the surfaces dry smooth and clean and sit nicely by the birds' legs—stones of separation, we call them as we project the chick's hypothetical lifeline, its probability of death during every step from embryo to hatchling. The funny thing is female albatrosses in successful breeding pairs are more likely to suffer from global warming than those who failed to breed, which we think is terribly romantic—sacrificing livelihood in the name of love. But our birds will be together for life, their feet glued to cardboard platforms, cardboard platforms fixed to a table, us fixed to our spots adhering layer over layer until the wire legs and masking tape and wadded balls of magazines disappear, our falsified organs, veins, toothpick bones providing an imaginary foundation, because without organs, there's no need for nutrients, colder waters bringing nitrogen from the deep end of the ocean, kelp seeping it up, females breeding to die or dying to breed and instead riding the breeze with their wings locked and extended, though we haven't figured out how to get the paper to dry beyond stiffness yet.

Lucy Zhang writes, codes, and watches anime. Her work has appeared in *CRAFT*, *The Spectacle*, *Redivider*, and elsewhere. She is the author of the chapbooks *Hollowed* (Thirty West Publishing) and *Absorption* (Harbor Review). Find her at https://lucyzhang.tech or on Twitter @Dango_Ramen.

ESSAYS & INSIGHTS

IN PRAISE OF THE HYBRID

LYNN MUNDELL

If micros are the carry-on luggage of fiction—carefully packed with the essentials; chosen for the quick entrance and exit—hybrid micros are the travel pet carriers in which something untamed lurks. This makes the hybrid writer also a curiosity. What's in that small container of yours? A memory or a story? Or something even wilder, such as an erasure poem in the shape of a small rabbit. Where are you going with it? And, most pressing, *why?*

Writers of hybrids—a literary genre most succinctly defined as blending two or more genres—may struggle in placing their little creatures, since there have been fewer journals and presses publishing non-traditional pieces. It may take longer to find a literary community. The writing can be difficult and dicey, as one crosses borders and boundaries while hewing to the heart of a piece.

But readers don't care about all of that. They are waiting for the goods, which good hybrids deliver. From strange and sometimes rough travels come unusual wonders: linked tales coated in the sandy film of childhood; spiced words uncorked to make a pattern across the page; tiny stories contained in Google Map directions.

In the twelve years I read more than 11,000 submissions while co-editing *100 Word Story* (an online literary journal that is exactly what it says it is), I enjoyed the gifts of many individual micros. But I treasured just as much the overall big picture of the changing landscape of short-short stories.

As a reader turned poet morphing into an essayist evolving into a flash writer, I was heartened to see how micros can be category defying. As a writer with no genre homeland, I found my own place among others' undefinable writing. Over the years, I saw memories of families taken apart, examined, and assembled into marvelous Frankenstories— poemy stories and storyish poems. I saw an entire wave of pandemic micro memoirs conjoined with science fiction or romance. I witnessed how with time the traditional tales seemed to be relaxing in their retelling—until the essays submitted to us read like stories, and vice versa, and the paths while still short at 100 words opened up to limitless vistas.

Overall, I've seen more journals loosening their descriptions of what they publish and writers celebrated for these works, with readers embracing pieces that move aside barriers of form to perfectly express what urgently needs saying. Just a few examples include Kathy Fish's "Collective Nouns for Humans in the Wild" from *Jellyfish Review*, referred to alternately as a poem, a story, and an essay and discussed everywhere from Reddit to YouTube; Kim Magowan's 100-word gem *"Madlib"* in Okay Donkey Magazine and later anthologized; and Audrey Bauman's "Adapted from the Merriam-Webster Dictionary's Definitions of 'Rock'," a hybrid using fable, a story and a specific form that won its *CRAFT* award in the broader flash fiction category. And, while journals such as *Bending Genres* from the get-go committed to publishing hybrids, other, conventional publications have increasingly added the genre to their pages.

Why the growing acceptance of hybrids? Maybe it's that as our own identification of ourselves opens—he, she, they, ze—so too does our storytelling. It could be that the world is changing at lightning speed, so we need literary forms mirroring that, which is why I felt spurred this year to create the online journal *Centaur* dedicated to the hybrid micro, which I hope writers and readers will keep redefining. Or perhaps it's that as the overall genre of flash fiction grows, with an increasing number of writers and readers, the hybrid genre (or non-genre, if you will) is finally coming into its own and revealing just how far and wide the short form can go.

When we read, we want to be inspired, entertained, surprised, or even all three at once, as I was with the very first hybrids I devoured: comic books. Hybrids tap into our independent spirit. As the writer Tania Hershman said, "Hybrid writing is, by its nature, writing that doesn't want you to say what it is." Recently I read a news article about a tabby on an airplane escaping its carrier to roam the aisles, astonishing the rows of passengers strapped into their seats. No one was quoted as being displeased. Quite the opposite. When the unusual breaks loose, rubs against our ankles, startles us from our slumber, we all feel an exhilarating jolt—a new definition.

WRITING IN ONE BREATH

EPIPHANY FERRELL

I write at the computer—it's how I outrun the inner critic. I try not to edit as I write. That's a separate process, mostly—for when I agonize over a paragraph break or whether it's OK to use a word like "very" when "very" is what I mean.

A blank page is a scary thing, sometimes. That's one reason I like to work from word prompts—the page isn't blank. And I have a first-go time limit—thirty minutes. That's just enough pressure to force something to happen, not enough time to overthink it. It's writing in one breath.

I like to examine the prompt-word list, then go away for fifteen minutes or so. I try to let my subconscious make connections between the words. If it's not happening, that thirty-minute time limit lets me off the hook. If it's going well, I keep writing until right before I run out of steam—taking Hemmingway's advice: ". . . always stop when you are going good and when you know what will happen next."

But here's the thing—you can't be afraid of a bad first draft. You can't be afraid to write sloppily, or produce something maudlin or prim or thin.

When I write from word prompts (or headlines, as with the potato story), it's inevitable I'll write myself into a hole sometimes. I'll take an absurd turn in the story, or bend a noun into a verb and shove it into the last sentence. But there, it's done, I've used all the words—and maybe it even worked.

The more days in a row I free-write from prompts, the easier it is to stretch. I become more limber. Words present themselves in a more pliant, mischievous way.

Which makes it all that much harder not to take it personally when, after a few good days—when writing is fun and the ideas flow like they are coming from somewhere outside—I hit a wall.

That's where the bad first draft comes in. It's skimming off the pond scum to reveal the goldfish moving in the water.

I find, that if I've had a few days of getting stuck, it helps to share the bad draft—a way to escort the elephant from the room.

I'm lucky to be part of a writing group that encourages first drafts. It's messy, creating is.

ON WRITING THE SAME OLD THING

FRANCINE WITTE

Most of my microfictions are about rotten boyfriends or rotten families. That's pretty much it. You pick up a Francine Witte story and that's the territory you are likely entering into. Oh sure, I'll throw in the occasional story about trees in a forest or people turning into trees in a forest (I love turning things into other things), but for the most part it's bad love and bad homelife. I can't help but wonder if it's okay to keep telling so many stories about the same damn thing.

And I can't help but wonder if you worry about this in your writing. You may have written about your car always breaking down or how you hate grocery shopping so you want to write something new. Something IMPORTANT. Something with relevance beyond you and your day-to-day travails. You start out writing about gun control or overpopulation and somehow you end up with your characters glaring at soup cans in Aisle 6. In my case, no matter what I start writing, I'm likely to end up with my father smashing his fist in a wall.

Someone the other day was referring to one of my stories and said, "You know, it's the one where your father smashes his fist through the wall." I said, "Well that's actually many of my stories." "Yeah," he said, "yeah."

If I'm not writing about fist-smashing, I'm writing about cheating, being left, a broken home, etc. And Dear God, how many stories have I written about Harry? It doesn't matter that there is no actual Harry, I can't stop writing about him.

It comes down to this—you gotta write what's yours. You must write the stories only you can write. And it doesn't matter how many times you tell it or even if it's true (my father never smashed a wall, but would glaring at my mother have been as interesting?).

The difference is nuance and execution. Not the *what* of the story, but the *how*. Adding something new to the old. There are so many things that change a story. Think Boy meets Girl and all the combinations and permutations that come from the one tiny plot. Even change Boy meets Girl to Girl meets Boy. See how easy that is?

So let's say, (and I'm saying this for myself, too) that if you like a theme, a topic, whatever and you think you've written about it too much, don't worry. Because no matter how old a story is to you, when your reader picks it up for the first time, to them, it's new.

MINI INTERVIEW WITH BRETT PRIBBLE

GHOST PARACHUTE

> *Ghost Parachute* published four of the stories
> included this year. Here, we ask Brett Pribble,
> Founding Editor of *Ghost Parachute*, a few
> questions about publishing microfiction.

What makes for a successful micro?

A lot of the same things that make a story of any
length successful. The writer doesn't just explain
the character's feelings. They put the character in a
situation and describe the character dealing with it.
It shouldn't just be a description of mundane tasks.
There need to be stakes. A good micro doesn't have
to provide us with all the answers, but it does need
to pack a punch.

> *Can you list some mistakes, craft-wise, that would*
> *reduce a story's chance of being published in* Ghost
> Parachute?

There is the standard stuff like not using correct
dialogue formatting, but I guess if the story is all
abstract language, and there is no sensory imagery

to ground the reader, that would lessen its chances.

Have you been seeing an increase of microfiction in your submissions queue? If so, to what do you attribute this growth?

Yes. Micros have become a lot more accepted in the literary community over the past few years. Literary journals publish microfiction more now than they ever have before. Seven years ago, when I said I was publishing microfiction, other writers often either didn't know what it was or said it was not real writing. People have finally come to understand that good writing doesn't need to have a high word count.

What do you want writers to know before they submit to Ghost Parachute*?*

To not be afraid to go to uncomfortable places. *Ghost Parachute* revels in stories many might think are too strange or dark to be published. Microfiction began as an experiment, so don't be afraid to experiment with yours.

BEST MICROFICTION THANKS THE JOURNALS WHERE THESE PIECES APPEARED IN 2022.

ALL MATERIAL USED BY PERMISSION.

"Her Mother, My Mother" by Hema Nataraju from *100 Word Story*.

"Jack and Jill's Final Adventure" by Epiphany Ferrell from *805 Lit + Art*.

"Knocking" by Tommy Dean from *Alternating Current Press*.

"A Field Guide to Prehistoric Motherhood" by Shelly Jones from *Apex Magazine*.

"Holy War" by Brett Biebel from *Atlas and Alice*.

"Cat Barbecue" by Tim Craig from *Atticus Review*.

"The Fox" by Bishop V. Navarro and "Your Childhood Best Friend Gets Her Hands on Some Questionable Dope" by Jasmine Sawers from *beestung*.

"Chiltepin" by Lynn Mundell and "Kindling" by Keith J. Powell from *Bending Genres*.

"The Extinction Museum: Exhibit #506 (Home Pregnancy Test, c. Early 2000s)" by Tina May Hall from *Big Other*.

"Tusks" by Ross McMeekin and "Hardy Holds Court at the Corner Store" by Kristina T. Saccone from *Cease, Cows.*

"Tattoos" by Jamy Bond and "Occur" by Judith Osilé Ohikuare from *CHEAP POP.*

"When You're the Contortionist" by Candace Hartsuyker from *Cleaver.*

"Stay as Long as You Need" by Slawka G. Scarso from *CLOVES Literary.*

"Attaboy Louis" by Shastri Akella from *CRAFT.*

"When the Cowboy Separates the Calves for Tomorrow's Branding" by Sabrina Hicks from *Emerge Literary Journal.*

"Unstable Relationship" by Lucy Zhang from *Exposition Review.*

"Owen Will Tell You" by Francine Witte from *Five South.*

"Via Combusta" by Sara Fetherolf from *Flash Boulevard.*

"Home" by Matt Barrett and "Warmer Water" by Mathieu Cailler from *Flash Frog.*

"What We Believed" by D.E. Hardy and "54.7754° N, 31.7890° E, April of 1940" by Slawka G. Scarso from *FlashBack Fiction.*

"Windows" by Elizabeth Maria Naranjo and "Bone on Bone" by Eric Scot Tryon from *Fractured Lit.*

"Visitacion Valley, 1962" by Patricia Q. Bidar, "Everything Depends on the Potato" by Epiphany Ferrell,

"Karol's Cleaners Will Clean Anything" by James R. Gapinski, and "banana boat" by Aureleo Sans from *Ghost Parachute*.

"An Eight Foot Possum" by Evan Williams and "The Circle Is A Part of the Hole" by Evan Williams from *Heavy Feather Review*.

"My Uncle Lived in the Future" by Parth Shah from *hex*.

"Long After the Long Ride into the Sunset" by Marvin Shackelford from *Janus Literary*.

"What the Mirror Tells You" by Gail Louise Siegel from *MicroLit Almanac*.

"A Solid Contribution" by Kathy Fish from *Milk Candy Review*.

"What I Owned" by Michelle Ross from *Monkeybicycle*.

"Groceries" by Tucker Leighty-Phillips from *Moon City Review*.

"24 Hour Elevator" by Ryan Griffith and "Workshop" by Kathleen McGookey from *New World Writing Quarterly*.

"Grease and Feathers" by Leila Martin from *Nurture: A Literary Journal*.

"The Deaths of the Great Lakes" by Jeffrey Hermann and "My Mother Visits Me in America and is Offended by What the Dishwasher Can Do" by Tara Isabel Zambrano from *Okay Donkey Magazine*.

"An Empty Day" by Pamela Painter from *Pangyrus*.

"9 Dystopias" by Monica Louzon, "Selected Google Searches Regarding Peter Jackson's King Kong" by Abigail Oswald and "rice & sugar" by Camil Piperni from *Paranoid Tree Press*.

"Cure for Tears" by Avra Margariti from *Pidgeonholes*.

"That Vasectomy Talk" by Sean Ennis and "Warmup" by E.J. Schwartz from *Pithead Chapel*.

"21 Allen Drive" by Diane Gottlieb from *SmokeLong Quarterly*.

"Sorrow Everywhere" by Pamela Painter from *South Florida Poetry Journal*.

"To You When You're Twelve and You Hate Yourself:" by Erica Frederick and "Alight" by Leila Renee from *Split Lip Magazine*.

"A Piece of You" by Diamond Braxton and "Potential" by Sabrina Hicks from *Stanchion*.

"Luck/History" by C.C. Russell from *takahē*.

"The Dream He Forgot" by Marzia Rahman from *The Antonym*.

"Available in Standard Sizes" by Christopher Notarnicola from *The Baltimore Review*.

"Snapper" by Nicholas Mainieri and "A Queer Girl's Guide to Reading Fairy Tales" by Rebecca Turkewitz from *The Cincinnati Review*.

"The Romantic Maneuvers of a Tilting Planet" by Tommy Dean and "Shine in Her Light" by Sabina Y. Wong from *The Citron Review*.

"Centaurs in the Laundromat" by Lynn Mundell from *The Disappointed Housewife*.

"By the Sea" by Faye Rapoport DesPres from *The Dribble Drabble Review*.

"Laugh Track" by Maria Robinson and "Squash" by Michelle Ross from *The Forge Literary Magazine*.

"My Mother's Dress Shop" by Jeff Friedman from *The Fortnightly Review*.

"Mr. Boggins" by Tucker Leighty-Phillips from *The Journal*.

"The Knife Thrower's Daughter" by Frankie McMillan from *The Phare*.

"The Beach" by Matt Barrett, "Dad Paddles In" by Teddy Engs, and "stamps" by Aureleo Sans from *trampset*.

"El Deliveryboy" by Christine Arroyo from *Variety Pack*.

"Last Time" by Douglas A. Wright from *Vestal Review*.

"What Bones Carry" by Janna Miller and "I'm a Honda Odyssey, I'm a Chrysler Voyager" by Eric Scot Tryon from *Whale Road Review*.

"From Yoyo" by Janelle Bassett, "Breath" by Bruce Johnson, and "The Final Girl Prepares to Watch Her Season of *American Horror Story*" by Megan Phillips from *Wigleaf*.

"Artificial Autonomy" by Helena Pantsis from *Wyld-blood (Wyld Flash)*.

112 Harvard Ave #65
Claremont, CA 91711 USA

pelekinesis@gmail.com
www.pelekinesis.com

Pelekinesis titles are available through Small Press
Distribution, Ingram, Gardners, and directly from the
publisher's website.

CPSIA information can be obtained
at www.ICGtesting.com
Printed in the USA
JSHW020924160623
43338JS00004B/23